Bound by an Angel

Mackenzie McKade

Samhain Publishing, Ltd.
11821 Mason Montgomery Road, 4B
Cincinnati, OH 45249
www.samhainpublishing.com

Bound by an Angel
Copyright © 2013 by Mackenzie McKade
Print ISBN: 978-1-61921-404-0
Digital ISBN: 978-1-61921-312-8

Editing by Sue Ellen Gower
Cover by Angela Waters

First Samhain Publishing, Ltd. electronic publication: October 2012
First Samhain Publishing, Ltd. print publication: December 2013

Praise for Mackenzie McKade's
Bound by an Angel

"Every time I read a Mackenzie McKade book I reaffirm the fact that I think she can write an amazingly hot story, she can bring to life the characters and she can also deliver a story I am interested in reading and connect with."

~ *Under the Covers Book Blog*

"This was number three in *Ties That Bind* series and an excellent addition. Loved Clancy, he is rugged, full of swagger, but oh so vulnerable when it comes to Tess. [...] Absolutely a must read."

~ *Sensual Reads*

"Mackenzie McKade has written a realistic and touching story about loss and the power of love in the healing process. [...] I can't wait to re-read this story and am already looking forward to the next installment in this series."

~ *Guilty Pleasures Book Reviews*

Look for these titles by
Mackenzie McKade

Now Available:

Dedication

To Sharis Mayer for once again lending me her friendship and support. I want to give a special thanks to Kelly Anderson whose friendship, insight and guidance helped me to pull Clancy's story together. Thank you.

Chapter One

"What the hell—"

Tess Gilmore held back her curse when she saw her two younger sisters peering through the heavy curtains at whatever was making that horrible racket. One might have called it singing if one had a tin ear. To Tess it sounded like a wolf caught in a trap or maybe a bear clearing its throat. And because she just happened to be the new choirmaster at Alabaster Elementary School, she knew a good voice when she heard one.

This was *not* one of them.

In the background the television hummed. Outside, the beat of bass drums throbbed so loud it rattled the windows. Country music blared as someone tried their best to sing Garth Brooks' song *Friends in Low Places*. Tess cringed when the vocalist attempted a note too high for his baritone voice.

Face buried between the curtains, her sister, Rachel, beckoned Tess with several quick waves of her hand. "Oh my God. You have to see this." The fair-haired beauty snorted. "I think it's our next-door neighbor. Judging by the way he's swaying while dancing on our retainer wall, I'd say he's drunk as a skunk."

Clancy Wiseman?

Tess had heard the naughty rumors about *that* cowboy. The stories told were deliciously sinful. But of course, she wouldn't dare get involved with a rogue who was known for dabbling in a little bondage and even more wicked adventures like threesomes. Their brother, Levi, had warned them all about the man who occupied the ranch next to them.

Still, curiosity had its claws in her. Tess quickened her steps until she eased behind Rose, the youngest of the identical twins by two minutes and the most forward and daring out of the two girls.

Grinning from ear to ear, her blue eyes laughing, Rose stared up at Tess. "Isn't he handsome?"

Tess gazed through the black curtain of night hampered only by truck lights that almost blinded her. She could barely make out the shadowy shape that teetered on the three-foot stucco fence.

Her sister's words drew Tess up short. "How do you know he's handsome?" How indeed?

Both girls' tittering stopped abruptly.

Tess shook her head. "Tell me you haven't been nosing around his property?"

Their meddling would be the death of her. At fifteen they were spreading their wings and soaking up as much independence as they could. Add an almost nineteen-year-old brother and—

The burden of her guardianship swept over Tess. Her chest tightened. Levi would be going off to college in less than a year. That is if she could keep him away from the girls. The last thing she needed to deal with was an unexpected marriage proposal or, God forbid, a pregnancy.

And Rose and Rachel—

"Well..." Rachel began, pushing aside her waist-length blonde hair that matched both Rose's and Tess's, while her twin finished her sentence, "it was a small peek. The girls at school say he is the most sought out cowboy in all of San Antonio, maybe even all of Texas. Who knows, maybe the world."

How was that for exaggeration?

"You two shouldn't be listening to idle gossip," Tess chastised.

The trouble was she had heard the same rumors. Not only was the man said to be tall, dark and handsome, but rich. Which was evident by his holdings, an impressive Spanish manor that sat on two thousand acres of prime land. His sullied reputation would only make him that much more attractive to some.

Certainly not her.

Tess had her family and career to think about. A randy cowboy was not in her plans. Tears came from out of nowhere to dampen her eyes. She quickly blinked them away before her sisters could see her sorrow. In all honesty, a year ago Tess wouldn't have thought twice about taking on a man like Wiseman, but not now, not since her parents' death. Her siblings relied on her. She had to set the standards so that they grew up in the environment their parents had set for them.

Tess eased back so the cowboy was no longer in her sights. "Get away from there. Maybe he'll just go home."

"Or pass out." Rachel chuckled, before parting the curtains once more and staring into the darkness. Rose joined her as Tess stepped away.

Clancy Wiseman.

Tess exhaled slowly, glancing around the large room, taking in its comfortable leather couch, love seat, and two matching chairs positioned before a large, stone fireplace. Angus Cattle Ranch, the Gilmore's new home, sat on seven hundred acres. While not as grandiose as Wiseman's, the two-story log cabin was spacious and homey. The scent of mesquite burning in the grate lent truth to its warmth.

She released a sigh of longing.

If only their parents hadn't died in a car accident a year ago. At twenty-three, she had never thought her life would take

11

such a drastic turn. She wasn't equipped to raise her sisters and brother. But then, when did anything make sense?

The change of scenery had been her suggestion. The move to San Antonio had been her brother's idea.

Levi had always dreamed of owning his own ranch and there was plenty of room for Rachel and Rosie to kick up their heels. But when he left for college, because no matter how he fought, he was getting a degree, the care of the ranch would fall upon her shoulders.

God. She should have thought this through better.

"Oh no!" Rose reared back, eyes wide with concern. "He fell."

All three of them rushed to the front door, but it was Tess who got there first. Back against the cool wood, she spread her arms out wide to bar the way. "No you don't. I'll take care of this." Her demand was met with a choir of disapprovals.

"Please, Tess, can't we come with you?" Rachel asked.

"Absolutely not. It's late. You both should be in bed. You have school tomorrow."

"Puleeezzze…" Rose whined, while Rachel echoed her.

"No. Now upstairs with you both." Tess waited a heartbeat before she pivoted, turned the porch light on and opened the door to step outside.

Dressed in old flannel pajamas and no robe, she crossed her arms beneath her full chest and hurried toward where she had last seen the man waltzing along the retainer wall. The wet grass beneath her bare feet chilled her. She should have returned for slippers, but concern kept her on track. His singing had stopped and that couldn't be a good sign.

I hope the idiot didn't hurt himself. Then again, it would serve him right. What was he doing here anyway?

Tess peeked over the wall. "Mr. Wiseman?"

Lying prone, he didn't move.

Her heart stuttered. *Oh God. Was he breathing?* Her pulse took flight as she quickly crawled over the abrasive stone wall. Kneeling so that her heels touched her butt, she placed her fingertips to his neck just beneath an obstinate jawbone and felt for life.

Thump. Thump. Thump.

Okay. So he wasn't dead, but he might as well be. The man appeared to be out cold. He smelled of whiskey, spicy cologne and a heady mixture of masculinity that she didn't want to affect her, but it did. Her pulse picked up a beat of temptation. She willed herself to look at him as an inconvenience, but the lock of dark hair that swept across one eye called to be brushed back. Before she knew it she reached out and her fingertips skimmed his forehead.

"What on God's green earth am I going to do with you?"

The only good thing about this situation, the cowboy's inebriated state, granted Tess the opportunity to really look at the man who had provoked so many rumors. Moonlight and headlights bathed his face in shadows, giving him a mysterious and sexy mien. In didn't help that the truck radio switched over to a dreamy love song. A steel guitar whined softly in the background.

Clancy Wiseman really was tall, dark and definitely handsome.

She sighed.

Long, black eyelashes lay like crescents atop his cheeks. A five o'clock shadow was rough beneath her gentle caress as she stroked her palm over his bristly cheek. He didn't wear a jacket, only a damp T-shirt that stretched over a broad chest and a firm muscled abdomen, and an impressive set of bulging biceps. Those enticing veins that ran up a healthy man's forearms had always turned her on, and then there were his hands. Large. Strong.

Tess shuddered, wondering what they would feel like against her skin. She inhaled the scent of him again, before she slowly continued her perusal.

Hmmm...

Tight blue jeans didn't hide the fact the man had what was needed to keep a woman satisfied. She swallowed hard. It had been one difficult year of celibacy. Maybe that's why she wasn't surprised by the image that suddenly filled her head.

Her. Him. Wrapped in a hot embrace. His firm body pressed against hers and his cock spreading her wide, filling her inch by delicious inch. She trembled, closing her eyes and reveling in the stolen moment of arousal. That familiar tingle in each nipple felt so good as it radiated throughout, making her breasts grow heavy before it moved lower.

"*Oomph...*" Air rushed out of Tess's lungs as she was suddenly grabbed and jerked forward. With a thud and a little squeal of bewilderment, she landed spread-eagled atop the cowboy, nose to nose.

Half-shuttered, dark eyes stared up at her.

"Are you an angel?"

His rich, deep voice slid across her like a sensual touch, sending a shiver up her spine, a fact that irritated the crap out of her. Tess didn't need any more complications in her life, and this man screamed of complications.

"No!" Pushing and shoving followed her sharp reply.

Any attempts to break his hold were fruitless. The man was strong. She wasn't a lightweight. At five-nine, she could hold her own. Well, usually.

His nose nudged hers. "Did you fall from Heaven?" Lips a breath away from hers tempted her, but she wasn't a fool. Before she could laugh at his audacity and put him in his place, he continued, "Will you be my angel tonight? Take me home?

Make love to me?" His breathy request made her eyelids rise swiftly.

"Absolutely not!"

Just the thought of being with this man caused her composure to waver and she couldn't allow that to happen. This was a new town, new beginnings, and for her family she needed to keep her reputation stellar. She'd left her wild life behind. Her family needed her. Just being in this cowboy's presence could ruin her.

Tess wiggled, but the movement only lodged his impressive bulge, the one she had shamelessly admired only moments ago, firmly against the pulse between her thighs.

Everything inside her went haywire. Her breathing became short, shallow intakes. Her nipples drew taut, while something low in her belly tightened uncomfortably. Chills raced across her flesh. Sadly, the prickling had nothing to do with the weather.

Desire.

Frustration left her lungs in a rush of air. "Mr. Wiseman, release me."

"But then I might miss the opportunity of a lifetime." His mouth brushed hers.

"This is ridiculous—" Before she could finish her sentence, he silenced her with a kiss.

Where Tess expected a wet, slobbery attempt to seduce from a drunken cowboy, she got just the opposite. The way he moved his warm lips tentatively over hers was meant to tempt and conquer. But she had to give herself credit. She clenched her jaws and struggled again for release. He nipped her bottom lip and she gasped. His tongue swept inside, sliding against hers. He hesitated a moment, and damned if her errant tongue didn't seek his. When she entered his mouth to taste him she was lost.

Fight gone. Vanished.

Desire unleashed.

It had been way too long since Tess had found comfort in a man's arms. Thought about her needs instead of those of her family.

The soft whimper she heard was her own. He sipped from her lips as if he savored a fine wine, before flicking his tongue against hers and then smoothing it over every inch of her mouth. The bitterness of whiskey blended with the thrill of a man who knew how to kiss.

Tess should put an end to this madness, but the cowboy beneath her stole her resistance. Besides, what would he remember in the morning? His memory would be sketchy at best. Still it seemed wrong to take advantage of him.

When his hands slid beneath her shirt, stroking her back, a tremor snaked through her. Work-callused palms glided over her flesh. One hand skimmed the underside of a breast. As lightning exploded through her now heavy globes, another moan escaped.

"Tess? Do you need our help?"

Rose's concern stopped Tess cold. She yanked upright, out of the cowboy's arms, her head popping up over the wall to see both her sisters standing at the door, staring in her direction.

Damn them. No. Damn her. She was at fault here.

Tess knew better than to dally with this man. Any man. There was too much to lose. Pushing to her feet, she glanced downward. The cowboy's grin as he threaded his fingers together behind his head made her growl with frustration. She snapped her attention back to her sisters.

"No. No. I've got everything under control." The knees of her pajamas were damp. Her bare feet were starting to freeze.

Yeah. I've got everything under control. Not.

"Get up," Tess muttered beneath her breath.

"Oh baby, I *am* up." The slow southern draw dripped like warm honey, sweet and enticing.

No. Tess wouldn't fall into his trap. Even with that said, she couldn't help it. She glanced down at his crotch and her eyes widened.

Yup. The man was up. The bulge hard to— No. Impossible to miss.

Wiseman reached for her and she slapped his hand away.

"Stop that." Tess turned her attention to her sisters who were slowly working their way toward them. "Stay there, girls. I said I've got this under control." But it was far from being under control. Her body ached for fulfillment and the man stroking her ankle wasn't helping. She stumbled back. "Get up—"

No, she wasn't going there. There was no telling what his response would be and she had to think about her sisters.

Wiseman made an attempt to stand, but fell back down. "Angel, I think I need your help."

Biting the inside of her cheek, Tess glared at him. What were the odds the man wasn't as drunk as he appeared? Would he remember their kiss?

"Yeah. Sure." Tess leaned down, shoving her arms beneath his armpits. "On three. One. Two. Three." With a hefty tug he rose, falling straight into her arms. When she attempted to release him, he held on tight.

Burying his nose in her hair, he inhaled. "Hey, Rose and Rachel."

Her sisters took his words as an invitation to join them. They hurried toward them.

Tess jerked back so that she stared into his eyes. "You know my sisters?" And if he recognized her sisters then he wasn't all that drunk.

Bastard.

"*Mmmm*... I'd rather get to know you better."

17

God. Tess hoped her sisters didn't hear that.

"Hi, Clancy," Rose cooed.

Rachel batted her eyelashes.

Her sisters were growing up way too fast.

With a grunt, Tess yanked free from his grasp. "Mr. Wiseman was just leaving." The sooner she got rid of him the better.

"Tess!" Both girls cried out at once, but it was Rose who continued. "You *can't* let him drive."

"No. Please." Big tears bloomed in Rachel's troubled eyes, but the fear in her voice was what chilled Tess.

It had been a drunken motorist who had killed their parents. And what made it even worse was the girls were right. Tess couldn't let the cowboy drive. It would be as irresponsible of her as it was for him driving while impaired.

Damn. What a quandary.

If she drove his truck, she had no way to get back home short of walking. The distance and the heavy clouds hanging in the sky made this choice simply out of the question. Of course, she could invite him inside until Levi got home from studying at a friend's house. But that option would leave her with the man—alone. The girls had to get to bed because they had school. Of course, so did she. It was her first day and she had to make a good impression.

No *good* alternative appeared to exist.

Tess chewed on the inside of her cheek again. "Mr. Wiseman, my sisters are right." *You're going to regret this* rang in her head. "Would you mind coming inside? Our brother should be home soon and then we can get you and your truck safely home."

His six-foot frame swayed. "Clancy." Slipping a finger beneath her chin, he dragged her gaze to meet his. Electricity sparked with his touch.

Tess had to struggle not to pull away and reveal how he affected her. "What?" Her forehead furrowed.

"Call me Clancy."

When hell freezes over.

The awkward silence that stretched between them was cut short when Rose blurted, "For heaven's sake, Tess. Just call him Clancy and let's go inside. It's cold out here." She stomped her feet, shifting side to side, as she hugged herself. Rachel stood beside her twin doing the same little shuffle.

The girls were right. *Again.* It was freezing.

Through clenched teeth, she managed, "Please, Clancy." Tess hated the tremble in her voice. She spun on the balls of her feet and headed for the house.

Male laughter followed her.

And then, if things couldn't get worse, they did.

Apparently Clancy stumbled forward, because he bumped into her back. As he was going down, he grabbed for her and missed. Instead he caught a handful of her pajama bottoms and they followed him down to the ground.

Dumbstruck, for a moment she just stood there. Then she slowly did a little geisha walk, pivoting to glare upon the irritating cowboy at her feet. A cool breeze swept up her bare legs, reminding her she wore no panties. She briefly closed her eyes in disbelief. Could this evening suck any more? When she pinned her sights back on the man, laughter danced in his eyes.

"Oops." A sheepish grin spread across his face.

Thankfully her shirttails covered her—well, mostly hid her from his sight.

Her sisters tittering set Tess in motion. Carefully, she bent down so that she didn't flash the man at her feet, but the heat in his eyes that glowed beneath the porch light said it was too late.

Hot humiliation stung her cheeks. Even her throat felt itchy with discomfort. This just couldn't be happening.

Inhaling a deep breath, she yanked her bottoms up and stretched to her full height. She didn't dare another look at the cowboy as she spun around.

"Rachel, help him up. Rose, go turn that radio off and get his keys."

The screen door screeched as she jerked it open and stepped inside, before letting it slam behind her. Anxious to put distance between her and that damn man, she headed for the kitchen. The rich scent of coffee met her. She could use a cup to warm her up. When she reached into the cupboard, her hands were shaking.

"Don't let him get to you," she chastised herself. But the male laughter in the living room only made her angrier, or was it embarrassment that soared? With quick, sharp movements she extracted two mugs and reached for the pot. Steam curled from the hot liquid as she poured.

When the doorbell rang, Tess let out an exasperated breath. "What now?" she mumbled.

Carrying the two mugs of coffee, she exited the kitchen, pulling up short when her gaze met tawny brown eyes filled with mischief.

Chapter Two

Ty Peterson's timing sucked.

Clancy looked through whiskey-shrouded eyes at his best friend's younger brother. When his truck broke down in front of the Gilmore's ranch, Clancy hadn't known who to call. Wade and Jessie would already be abed. He'd taken a stab in the dark that Ty wasn't. The soft giggling in the background said he'd been wrong. But at least he was awake.

But friends were friends and Clancy was glad to count Ty one of them. Well, most the time. The damn man's heated gaze hadn't left the shapely blonde standing before them with two cups of steaming coffee in her hands.

"Where's your manners, Wiseman? Introduce me to these three lovely ladies?" Ty rubbed his thumb and index finger slowly over his short-cropped mustache and bearded chin. His mouth curved into a sultry smile.

"I'm Rose." With rosy cheeks, she stepped forward with her hand outstretched.

The golden-brown-haired devil gave the older sister another interested once-over before he turned his full attention to the precocious teenager. "Ty Peterson, ma'am." After tipping his hat, he shook her hand. "Pleasure to meet such a pretty filly. And who is this exact replica?"

"Rachel." The young girl straightened her backbone, her chin rising slightly. "You know we're not actually identical. I'm a half inch taller than she is."

Rose huffed. "Really, Rachel?"

Ty gifted her with a roguish grin that Clancy had seen melt a woman's heart more than once. Then the scoundrel exchanged Rose's hand for Rachel's.

"Well, it's a pleasure to meet both of you." He planted a kiss atop her knuckles.

Rachel's baby-blue eyes sparkled as she threw a *ha-ha-I-got-a-kiss-and-you-didn't* look toward her sister.

Rose compressed her dainty little lips, not quite a pout, but close.

"Okay, girls, that's enough. Get on up to your rooms." The young woman with long, slender legs leading up to the most delicious hips and derrière Clancy had ever seen threw a nod in the direction of the stairs. "You have school tomorrow."

"Tess, what about hospitality?" Rose squealed.

"Yeah. It wouldn't be very hospitable of us to leave our company alone," Rachel chimed.

"They're not alone. I'm here." She paused, waiting.

Clancy half expected her to tap a foot impatiently.

Her sisters glared.

"Now." The firmness in her tone left no room for argument.

Grumbling, both girls said their good-byes and slowly headed for stairs. When they stopped at the bottom step, both looked backed longingly.

Tess's eyes widened. "Get!"

Then she turned those intense blue eyes on Clancy and something tightened in his chest. "Mr. Wiseman, I hope you take your coffee black." She handed him the steaming cup.

The damn thing nearly burnt his hand as he jostled it to where he could slip his finger through the handle. He hadn't noticed until then that his hands were nearly frozen. But the thought of this beautiful woman pressed against his body warmed him up as fast as the coffee had when he took a sip.

Memories of the kiss they shared made his cock twitch. Where would the caress have led them if her sisters hadn't interrupted?

"Mr. Peterson, care for coffee?"

"Don't mind if I do...*Tess*." Her name came out as a purr on Ty's tongue.

The woman handed the last cup she held to him, and then folded her arms beneath her large breasts. She had yet to ease the keenness in her eyes or her rigid stance.

"Apparently, the two of you know each other. So can I assume, Mr. Peterson, you are here to retrieve Mr. Wiseman and his truck?"

"Ty."

She blinked. "Excuse me?"

"Call me Ty."

An exasperated rush of air pushed between her kissable lips. From the frustrated look on her face, Clancy could imagine her thinking *not you too*.

"Ty. Have you come to rescue *Clancy*?" He smiled at the emphasis she placed on his name.

Ty glanced over at him. "Bro, do you need rescuing?"

"Not me." He took a sip of the hot coffee, feeling it warm him from the inside out.

"It's late, boys, and I have school tomorrow, so let's stop this merry-go-round because I need to get off."

The unconscious innuendo forced a slow grin upon Ty's face that matched his own.

It didn't make sense, but the moment Clancy had opened his eyes to the angelic beauty hovering over him, for whatever crazy reason, she had felt like a lifeline, the only thing keeping him from drowning in his sorrows as he lay upon the damp ground.

Damn. He ran his fingers through his hair. He must be drunker than he thought, or the nightmare that had driven him into the cold had affected him more than he wanted to admit. It was evenings like these that he wandered the night finding comfort in the depths of a whiskey bottle.

But now all he could think of was her long, shapely legs wrapped around his waist as she shattered in his arms.

Before either of them could say anything, she rolled her eyes. "Uhmmm. I didn't mean that quite the way it came out. It's just been a long night and it's time we all go to bed." Pinching her lips together, she fought the smile that twinkled in eyes so light blue he felt like he could melt into them.

Clancy saw the moment Tess regained her composure. Her gaze firmed along with her backbone. When she spoke again it sounded a little condescending, as if she were dismissing her sisters, instead of two adult men.

"It was a pleasure meeting you both, but it's getting late. I still have things in the kitchen to tend to before," she paused, "the evening is over. Feel free to finish your coffee and let yourselves out."

As she pivoted and disappeared into the kitchen, Clancy couldn't stop himself from taking several steps in her direction. Only when Ty said, "Holding out on me, Wiseman?" did he stop and turn around. His friend took a drink of his coffee, looking over the edge of the mug. "Not a nice thing to do. Not nice at all." Male interest stared back at Clancy and for some reason he didn't like it. Not one damn bit.

"Just met her tonight," he grumbled.

"Wouldn't mind taking that filly for a ride. Winding that long blonde hair in a fist and fuckin'—"

"Shut the fuck up." A red haze misted Clancy's sight. For some irrational reason he couldn't bear the thought of anyone, including a friend, speaking disrespectfully about the woman.

He pushed his fingers through his hair again and swayed, his footing unsteady.

Something pure and innocent shrouded her. Classical features, high cheekbones, creamy smooth skin, and lips that appeared sculpted and painted, reminded him of a porcelain doll.

Yeah. Tess Gilmore was too good for Peterson. Hell. What was he saying? She was too good for him.

Ty's eyebrows shot up. "Easy, Wiseman," he said softly, but his warning came through loud and clear. Unlike his brother Wade, Ty had an easygoing personality, but he still wasn't a man you wanted to screw with. None of the Petersons were.

Clancy retraced his steps, slapping Ty upon the back. "She's out of our league, buddy." Then he clasped the man's shoulder and gave it a playful shake. "According to her sisters she's the only thing their brother and them have. No other family." He released his friend. "Besides, she's a damn school teacher." A broken laugh slipped between his lips. "Tess Gilmore doesn't need the two of us screwing with her head."

Ty's silent scrutiny of him set Clancy on edge. Behind those knowing eyes the wheels were churning and he wasn't sure whether that was good or bad.

"Let's get the hell out of Dodge. I've got a couple bottles of whiskey in my truck calling our names. Shit!" He hesitated. "Damn thing stalled and won't start. I'll call a tow truck tomorrow."

"No problem. I'll tow you home. At least you won't have to come back here tomorrow." A mischievous grin fell across Ty's face.

"Fuck you," Clancy barked, and then he smiled.

Strolling over to the coffee table before the couch, he set his cup down as Ty followed suit. For a moment he thought of saying good-bye, but Tess had made it clear—his company wasn't welcome.

Probably for the best.

When Tess heard both the front and screen door open and close she breathed a sigh of relief. Pulling the plug from the sink, she watched the soapy water swirl and disappear down the drain. Uneasy laughter spilled from her mouth as she dried her hands.

"I need to get off. Did I really say that...out loud?" But getting off was just what she needed.

She folded the towel in her hands and laid it on the counter, realizing her body was still heated by Ty's and Clancy's roguish smiles. Their minds had made a beeline for the gutter and she'd followed them like a stray puppy. After the *it's time we all go to bed* comment, she quickly pulled her foot out of her mouth, regained what little composure she had left and nearly ran from the room. Well, maybe she didn't run, but she felt like it as thoughts of being sandwiched between the two men made her skin go up in flames. Sinking her hands into hot dishwater had done nothing to cool her arousal.

Tess looked around the kitchen, deciding nothing else needed to be done tonight, and exited the room. Her gaze glanced to the two cups sitting on the coffee table and she licked her lips. What would their mouths and hands feel like roaming her body? She had never had two men take her at the same time. Yes. It was a shameless fantasy, but what could she say? Didn't every woman dream of being worshipped by two men at once, or was she different?

As if she could erase the vision of two sets of lips and hands stroking her, Tess shook her head. She had to stop thinking like this. Clancy Wiseman was dangerous. Ty Peterson wasn't any better. She headed for the front door to check if the men had locked it when they left, when the doorknob turned.

Levi popped his sandy-blond head inside. "Sorry I'm late, sis."

Hands on her hips, she narrowed her gaze on his tall, athletic frame. "Don't let it happen again. I worry about you."

"I know." He entered, eyeing her warily from head to toe. "Were you wearing *that* without a robe for our company?"

So he had seen the cowboys leave.

At six-foot-two, it was difficult to look at her brother as a child, especially when his good looks beckoned every female from miles around. He had matured so much over the last year.

"As a matter of fact, yes." Tess held back the laughter bubbling inside her. His protectiveness was endearing, but unnecessary. Her pajamas were flannel, not the sexy baby doll ones she had hidden beneath her other lingerie. Of course, she couldn't help but wonder what he would say once their nosey little sisters spilled the beans about her losing her pants in front of Clancy.

"You know I've heard—"

"That's enough, Levi," she said firmly. "It isn't nice to listen to rumors. Mr. Wiseman's truck broke down in front of our house and Mr. Peterson was nice enough to help him."

"Which Peterson was that?"

She exhaled a heavy breath. "You mean there's more than one?" God, save the female population.

"Three brothers and a sister."

"I think he said his name was Ty." Who was she fooling? She would never forget that man and his sultry eyes sliding over her flesh like she was a strawberry-filled donut with cream on top.

Levi's brows furrowed. "*Hmmm.* Heard that Ty—"

Tess held up a hand, palm out, stopping her brother. "I shudder to think where you are hearing all these rumors.

Maybe I ought to take a closer look at who you're hanging around."

"Guys talk. And I was asking around about breeding. It appears Wiseman and the Petersons have some of the best stock in town. I thought this weekend I'd take a look. *Alone*," he added.

"Not on my dime, you won't."

"Tess," he groaned. "You don't know nothin' about horses and cattle. If I could negotiate breeding rights with—"

"And I won't learn anything unless I'm involved. When you leave I'll be running this ranch until you return." Well, more like managing it, because she would have to hire someone to help. Even still she wondered how she would accomplish it, but she was determined to make this place a home. Somewhere Levi could come back to when he finished school.

A sheepish expression flickered across Levi's face. "I was thinking—"

"Best you not think tonight and get to bed."

Levi didn't have to complete his sentence. It was the same argument. Her didn't want to go to college. He wanted to ranch. It was what he had always wanted. Their home in California had been horse property, so they were able to have a couple of horses, a cow and a handful of chickens, but that hadn't been enough for him. His dreams were bigger. He wanted to live the life of a *real* cowboy. And real cowboys raised, bred, herded and sold cows and horses.

After the death of their parents Tess found it difficult to refuse her siblings anything. Their sorrow had been so devastating, so heart wrenching, that they all needed a change of pace and scenery.

Levi quietly shook his head and headed for the stairs. On leaden feet she followed him up. She couldn't blame him for wanting to plunge head first into their new adventure financed by their inheritance, but if they failed, she would be at fault. Levi had to realize he needed something to back them up if that happened. Her meager wages as a schoolteacher would only stretch so far.

Her brother turned and took her in his strong embrace. "You worry too much," he muttered against her ear. "I love you, sis."

As moisture bloomed in her eyes, Tess thought she smelled the hint of alcohol, and then she remembered the beer she'd had after dinner. Attempting to blink the emotion away before Levi witnessed her weakness, she muttered, "I love you too." Much to her dismay, her voice cracked. She squeezed and released him, quickly turning away before he saw her tears. Above all things she had to stay grounded.

"'Night." His door shut with a click.

"Goodnight, Levi," she whispered.

Pausing at her bedroom, she glanced down the hall at her sisters' and brother's rooms. God. She hoped she made the right decision moving them to Texas. Taking a deep breath, she stepped inside her bedroom and closed the door, locking it and dimming the overhead lighting, before she pushed down her still damp pajamas bottoms, pausing to smile.

Clancy Wiseman was the devil reincarnated. Pure, unadulterated sin. Not to mention forbidden.

As she plucked at the buttons of her flannel shirt, the thought of the kiss they shared made her nipples bead into hard peaks. The soft material of her pajama top slid across sensitive flesh and a shiver raced up her spine.

That man could kiss. And his voice. Sultry. Wicked. And oh so enticing.

By the time her shirt joined her pants on the soft, gray carpet, tingles of arousal swept over her. Unthinking, she caressed her hands down her body, her palms shaping her breasts, abdomen and hips as she felt the warm pulse between her legs. Retracing the path upward, she cradled her heavy globes once again. With her thumbs and forefingers, she squeezed the tips, tossing back her head at the delicious ache that spread throughout.

Nights like this one she longed for the touch of a man. Instead, she moved to the nightstand next to her queen-size bed and picked up the channel changer. Turning on the television, she tapped in the secret code only she knew. In seconds the large screen hanging from the wall filled with the images of a naked man and woman locked in an embrace. A throaty moan eased from the shapely brunette's lips, while in the background seductive music played softly.

Tess watched the dark-haired man trail kisses down the woman's slender neck. She tilted her head, stretching her neck as if she could feel the gentle abrasion of the man's five o'clock shadow against her own skin, his moist lips and his hands smoothing up and down her back. With his back facing Tess, she imagined it was the sexy cowboy who had elicited such a hungry response in her earlier. Broad, impressive shoulders made her ache to reach out and feel the steely strength harnessed within, while the taut muscles in his ass flexed invitingly. Between parted thighs she glimpsed his testicles and her mouth watered.

What would Clancy taste like? Would he lose control if she took him deep in her mouth? Sucked. Long and hard.

Her breath caught as her pussy suddenly contracted. *Dammit.* All she was doing was tormenting herself. Still, when the man on the television caressed his mouth further south on the beautiful brunette, stopping to lick and tease the woman's luscious breasts, Tess found herself opening one of the drawers of her maple captain's headboard. Feeling around for the hidden latch, she pushed the button and the bottom slid open to display her own little treasure chest of toys. Gaze still pinned on the television screen, she grabbed her vibrator, the one with the clit stimulator.

As the man pushed the woman upon the bed, Tess eased upon the patchwork comforter, her head landing on a soft down pillow.

"*Are you an angel?*" The rich, masculine voice slid across her mind like silk.

Oh God. Now she was hearing things, because the guy on the screen was buried between the woman's legs, moaning and humming, not teasing Tess with the sexy words she had heard earlier.

Memories of Clancy's sensual request, "*Will you be my angel tonight? Take me home? Make love to me?*" parted her thighs. Her hand shook when she placed the vibrator at the opening of her swollen folds. She was so wet, slick, the toy slid in easily, filling her with cold satisfaction. Then she pressed the button and a rolling movement began inside her, pulsating against her sensitive clit to steal her breath.

"Yes," she hissed.

Drawing her attention back to the couple on the screen, she raised her hips, meeting each push of her hand. The man glanced up at the woman with a mischievous grin as he slowly crawled, rubbing his firm body along the brunette's lithe frame and easing his hips between her thighs.

Tess knew the moment he entered the woman, because the brunette arched her back, mouth parting on a whimper. Tess swallowed hard. She wanted to be that woman, wanted to be the one beneath that firm body, feel his rock-hard cock moving in and out of her of sex.

As a rosy areola disappeared in his mouth, Tess dragged her free hand up, finding a needy nipple, and pinched, sending electrical charges through both of her breasts. With a slide of a finger she increased the speed of the vibrator. The bunny ears stroked her clit with penetrating movements, causing her pussy to tighten. Her climax struck, hard and fast. She cried out. Heat surged, an echo of sensation pulsating throughout her body like a heartbeat. The exquisite moment left her breathing in small, shallow pants and her body trembling.

Slowly she dislodged the vibrator and placed it atop the nightstand before she switched the television and lights off. Rolling onto her side in the dark, she curled in a fetal position. That's when the tears began to fall.

She felt so alone.

Chapter Three

A pounding headache throbbing against his temples greeted Clancy in the morning. Squinting, he stepped out of his Spanish-style manor into the crisp cool air. Several white, cottony clouds hung in the blue sky, but it appeared the rain had headed west toward New Mexico judging by the grayness in that direction. Moisture was good for his fields, but too much of a good thing was wearing. He'd had enough of this wet weather.

Clancy squared his Stetson on his head and began to stroll toward the barn, relieved to discover his ranch hands had already fed the stock. Bundles of hay poked out of the wire bars of the feeders hanging along the pasture fence, while his cattle and horses chomped down on the sweet-smelling alfalfa. But what lingered in his mind was the clean scent of one woman. A woman who had decided to haunt his dreams last night.

The thought reined his mind in the direction of a tall, blonde beauty with the lips of an angel. He touched a finger to his lips. Damn. He couldn't remember when a woman had kissed him with such genuine passion, a hunger to match his own.

Then he chuckled.

Her expression when he yanked her pants down to her ankles had been priceless. Yet he'd paid for his misstep. When he'd struck the ground and looked up, his damn heart had nearly jumped out of his chest. His gaze followed those lovely long legs upward and discovered she wore no panties. All that creamy skin had lead up to a small landing patch of blonde, curly pubic hair he'd give his soul to explore.

What on earth was he saying? Tess Gilmore wasn't his type. He preferred a more experienced woman. Bodacious and adventurous. A woman who wasn't looking for a husband or the happily ever after, but one living for the moment and the excitement they could offer each other. No ties. No commitments.

Besides, the schoolmarm didn't need someone like him turning her quiet, peaceful, straight-laced world upside down. Not that she'd given him any hint she was interested. But there was that kiss they'd shared. No. It had to have been his alcohol-induced imagination. He was better off staying away from the beautiful schoolteacher for both of their sakes.

The heavy barn door squeaked as he pushed it open and entered the large, spacious building. The cement pathways along each stall had already been swept, clean straw replaced in each corral, and everything in its place. Organized. Neat.

Clancy almost laughed. On the outside his life appeared charmed, more than comfortable, but appearances were deceiving. The truth was he had nothing of real value, nothing that he held close to his heart. Well, except for Jessie, and he hadn't been able to hold on to her either.

A heavy sigh left his lungs, as Bella, his dapple mare, whinnied. He turned to where she stood, clawing the ground with a hoof and demanding his attention. The boys must not have given her oats this morning.

"Hey, girl." He ran a palm down her forehead to her soft nose. She twitched her whiskers, nuzzling his hand, while she made quiet grunting noises. "Until I find out whether you've eaten, no honey oats for you."

"Morning, boss." Clancy glanced over a shoulder to see Milo Green sauntering up beside him. "Is the wicked wench trying to get you to feed her again?"

"So she's had her oats?"

"Absolutely." The tall, lanky man pulled the gray mare's forelock. "Along with all the other hay-burners in this barn. She's just greedy like most women."

And Milo would know.

His young ex-wife had taken every penny he had saved, along with a two-year-old daughter, and ran off. At his own expense, Clancy had hired a detective to track the woman down. Milo deserved to have a relationship with his child. No one should be deprived of his or her family. Not like Clancy had.

"Heard anything yet?" he inquired.

Milo's face lengthened. "Not a thing." He pinched his lips together. "Guess I can only hope that Debbie is taking care of Julie. I miss her." His voice cracked before he quickly looked away. "I thought I'd ride the fence. Look for any downed trees. We had a pretty good downfall late last night."

"I'll take care of it." Clancy needed to do something to keep his mind off one delicious neighbor. "Is the quad gassed?" Instead of riding Bella, he'd take the all-terrain vehicle out. That way he could carry more supplies, including the chainsaw if he needed it.

"Yep. Already loaded too. You sure you don't want me to tag along?"

"Nah. I need the exercise." Work off some of the restless energy he'd acquired last night.

"Then I'll take a look at your truck. Should have it running by noon." Milo tipped his straw hat and wandered off as Clancy went into the connecting building where he kept his toys. Along with four matching ATVs there was a multipurpose utility vehicle, a motorcycle, a thirty-six-foot boat, and a shiny, black Jaguar.

Every man should have plenty of things to keep his mind occupied, he'd heard once. But *things* had never filled the emptiness in his life.

Grabbing one of the keys from the lockbox, he headed toward the vehicle containing his fencing equipment. With a tap of a button on the handle, the large garage door groaned as it climbed higher and higher. Throwing a leg over the bike and sitting down, he inserted the key and twisted. The engine roared to life. He eased his thumb against the gas lever and the quad shot forward.

He'd gone only a small distance when he heard someone yell, "You stubborn little bastard."

As his vehicle sprang beyond the brush, he saw the woman of his dreams with a branch in her hand swatting a midsize calf on the butt. Judging by the brand, a C and a lazy W lying on its side, it was one of his calves that had trespassed onto the Gilmore's property.

He pulled the vehicle to a stop and cut the motor. "Need some help?"

"I could have used your help when this thing trampled my sisters' garden and ate darn near a truckload of carrots," she hissed. "I still don't know how he got out." Tess was staring at Clancy and must not have seen the animal move, because when she swung again, the anger behind her swing launched her forward.

She screamed, falling.

Clancy jumped off the bike at lightning speed, but it didn't save the woman dressed in a navy-blue suit. She struck the puddle hard, raising a spray of grimy muck that flew in all directions.

Tess came up sputtering. By the icy shards sparking in her eyes, she was madder than a wet hen. She made several attempts to get to her feet, slipping and sliding, finally succeeding. But her struggle was only half over. As she tried to move beyond the puddle, sticky mud grappled with one of her feet, refusing to release her. She fought for several more seconds before relinquishing her shoe and stumbling to solid ground.

Fists and teeth clenched, she mumbled something he didn't understand, but her next words were clear as day. "That's it. You're dead," she growled, continuing to rave at the dumb animal that had found a patch of grass to nibble and ignore her. "I'll have your ass on the table for dinner tonight."

Clancy wasn't sure this was the right time to tell her the calf belonged to him. Cautiously, he placed a booted foot on the barbwire that had come loose due to a heavy tree branch that lay across it. Carefully he stepped upon Gilmore property.

She skimmed her gaze down the front of her and her expression fell. A heart-wrenching groan left her trembling lips. "I'll be late and it's my first day." Tears bloomed, threatening to fall, but she held them contained. "What am I going to do?"

"I'll take care of the calf and fence. You go clean up."

"I have to get this beast back in his pen." She wiped a hand across her cheek, spreading a streak of mud across her face.

The sight nearly made him laugh, but he stopped himself. Odds were if she saw his merriment, he might find *his* ass on her dinner table next to the calf.

"Uh. Tess. The *beast,* as you call him, happens to be one of mine."

"Yours!" Her eyebrows rose so high they almost touch her hairline. Her eyes widened before they narrowed to small slits spitting fire. "*Arghhh.*"

"As you can see, lightning struck that tree over there." He pointed to a singed, black trunk of a large oak tree. "Broke a branch clear in two. These things happen on a ranch, but I'll take care of everything."

Her mouth parted as if she planned to ream him a new asshole, then she spun around. On one shoe she limped away, her arms swinging with enough fury to propel her forward.

Clancy looked at the innocent calf still chowing down on his breakfast, clearly unconcerned about the theatrics revolving around him. Returning to his quad, Clancy slipped on his gloves and retrieved a rope before returning to capture the animal and lead him back over to his property. After quickly rigging a makeshift fence, he hurried to follow the woman's footsteps.

Cold mud seeped through Tess's clothing, sending a chill straight through her. What the hell had she gotten herself into? Standing on the back porch and covered head to foot in slimy guck, her body shook, barely holding back her tears, regrets and anger.

Who was she fooling?

She knew nothing about ranch life. Sure, they had animals in California, but this was on a larger scale, not just a hobby. She was a city girl—a teacher—not a rancher.

As she peeled off her soiled jacket, she wished Levi and the girls hadn't left early for school to pick up a couple of friends. Nothing was working out how she'd planned today. She shimmied her skirt over her hips and it slipped down her legs, falling to her feet. Stepping out of the mess, she kicked her foot, slinging the last of her expensive shoes across the wooden floor to slam against the house.

Damn Clancy Wiseman.

The large, black heifer casually making mincemeat of the girls' garden belonged to him. Rose and Rachel would be devastated when they saw the damage.

Looking down at her ruined silk shirt, Tess plucked at the buttons and jerked the garment off. For two cents she'd make Clancy pay for her soiled clothes and shoes. She cast a despairing glance toward where she had last seen him and froze. Her breath caught when she met intense eyes staring into hers. Tess hadn't even heard Clancy's approach, but she felt his heated gaze creep slowly up her nearly bare body.

"I just wanted to say I'm sorry." His deep, throaty voice slid across her skin, raising extra goose bumps.

First her pajama bottoms, now this. The way she was going, the next time they met she'd be stark naked.

Her modesty had already flown the coop. There was no use in trying to cover up. Still, it made her blush when she spun around, knowing he got a picture-perfect view of her derriere in the thong she wore. But as she moved across the porch to the backdoor, her foot landed on her silk shirt and *whish*. The slick fabric slid across the wooden floor, jerking her feet from beneath her.

She promptly fell on her butt with an *umph*.

The echo of booted steps pounded up the stairs and across the deck. Before she could catch her breath, strong arms assisted her to her feet and pulled her tight against a rock-hard chest covered in leather. The chill of the material seeped into her flesh.

She trembled.

"You hurt?" he asked.

"Only my pride." But that wasn't exactly true. Her ass throbbed from the impact. She'd probably have a nasty bruise and she was cold.

"You're shivering. Let's get you into the house." He turned the doorknob, but it wouldn't budge. "It's locked."

"Of course it's locked," she groaned, feeling completely defeated. "My keys are in my purse, which is sitting on the hood of my car." Which just happened to be in the front yard, where anyone driving by would catch a glimpse of her in nothing but her bra and thong.

Could this morning get any worse?

"I'll get your keys," he said.

Releasing her, he shrugged out of his coat and placed it around her shoulders. An all-masculine scent touched her along with an underlying hint of his cologne, a spicy concoction that almost made her melt in its embrace. She pulled the jacket closer around her. Partially because she needed the warmth it offered, and the other reason she'd rather not think about.

Without another word, he tracked back across the porch and disappeared around the corner, leaving her in silence and her own damn thoughts.

Yes, the man was chivalrous, but she had to remember she wouldn't be in this position if it weren't for him. And then there were those rumors that both frightened and intrigued her. She was still stressing when he returned.

"Here you go." Slipping the purse into her hands, he waited until she fished out her keys and handed them to him. Then he opened the back door and held it open so she could enter.

Expecting him to remain outside, she turned to thank him and smashed into his unyielding chest. His arms snaked around her to keep her from falling yet again.

"We have to quit meeting like this." He chuckled, his laughter dying when their eyes met. His darkened, while hers felt as if they were trapped in a seductive web of desire. He smoothed a large palm across her cheek. "Tess," he whispered. Bowing his head, he lowered his lips to hers.

Her mouth watered. She clenched her fingers around her purse, while her pulse thrummed like white lightning through her veins. But before he could kiss her, she gasped, ducking out of his arms.

"I gotta go." She snatched her keys from his hand. "Here." Slipping from his jacket, she pressed it into his hands, before she darted toward the archway leading into the living room. Hesitating, she briefly glanced over a shoulder. "I trust you'll ensure that no more of your animals do damage to my place?"

Clancy ran a thumb and forefinger along the rim of his Stetson. "Sure thing, ma'am." A smile twinkled in his sexy blue eyes.

Tess stepped through the opening and collapsed against the wall on the other side. Her heart beat so fast it made it difficult to breath. She heard him chuckle and the door close behind him.

The man was bad for her health.

Wasting no more time, she headed toward her room, tossing her purse on the bed along with the discarded outfits that hadn't made the cut this morning. If she hurried, maybe she wouldn't be too late.

Peeling off her bra and thong, she jumped into the shower and rinsed off. It only took seconds and she stood on the bathmat toweling dry. A few splatters of mud remained in her hair, but she'd brush it out when she got to school. Plucking the hairpins from the bun atop her head, she finger-combed the golden hair tumbling around her shoulders.

After donning underclothing, she grabbed the midthigh, plaid black, red and white skirt with the matching red sweater and quickly dressed. The clock next to her bed on the nightstand said time was ticking. Hopping on one foot, she slipped her other foot into a shoe and was out the door in a flash. Hollow heels slapped against the floor as she ran through the house and the front door, locking it before she headed for her car.

Getting into her vehicle, movement to her right caught her attention and she stopped midway. The groan rising in her throat died when she realized it was Clancy and not another pesky calf. On his hands and knees, he was attempting to put to right her sisters' garden. He raised a hand and waved. She offered the same before slipping behind the wheel and turning the ignition. As she sped down the driveway and out on the street, she realized something.

41

Perhaps there was more to her roguish neighbor then the bad boy rumors.

Chapter Four

Clancy stepped out of the windy afternoon into the warmth the elementary school offered. A plump, brunette administrator at the front desk raised her head at the sound of the door clicking shut behind him.

As he approached she smiled up at him. "Mr. Wiseman. How nice to see you. Here to pick up Shelby?"

Removing his Stetson, he gave the mid-forty-something woman a nod as he glanced at her nametag. "Sorry I'm late, Barbara." When he received Jessie's call to pick up her sister, he'd been twenty minutes away.

"Mrs. Peterson called ahead. Trailer of sick cows or something like that."

Jessie Evans, now Peterson since she married Clancy's best friend, Wade, had been his childhood friend and confidante. They shared a history of secrets. But she had been so much more than just a friend.

"Yeah. Sick cows," he murmured as his mind wandered.

When Jessie and he were younger, after one of Clancy's parents' explosive fights, they had made a pact never to marry. Later on, he, Jessie and Wade became friends with benefits. They had made the perfect threesome. No ties. No commitments. It worked for them, until his friends had fallen in love, leaving him alone and adrift.

"...Mr. Wiseman?"

"I'm sorry." He pulled his head out of his ass and focused on the woman before him. "You were saying?"

"Shelby is in her classroom, room 203."

"Thank you."

Hat in his hand, he headed down the carpeted hallway. Two rowdy boys ran past, almost running into him.

"Tyson and Jacob! Stop running," Barbara yelled.

Clancy didn't look around to see if the children had slowed. Instead he fell into a nostalgic moment as the familiar scent of wet paste rose. He stopped before a bulletin board littered with colorful construction paper artwork. A small smile tugged at the corner of his mouth. Front and center was Shelby's masterpiece.

From the moment the young girl had come into his life, she had taken to horses. He wasn't surprised to see a semblance of Digger in the middle of the picture. The big gray gelding had been a recent birthday gift from Tori, Wade's youngest sibling and only sister. A new horse blanket and bridle had come from Ty, while their eldest brother, Clint Junior, had purchased Shelby a saddle. Clint Senior and Madeline, their parents, had given the child an exquisite porcelain doll, which was so not like Shelby. But Madeline said every girl should have a doll and who would know better than the trauma counselor who had not only assisted Shelby in adjusting to her mother's tragic overdose and death, but her father's abandonment.

The padding of quick footsteps coming down the hall jerked Clancy out of his wanderings. He turned just in time for a small, dark-haired girl to fling herself into his arms. He swung her up, giving her a big hug.

"Clancy!" Shelby wrapped her arms around his neck. "I won," she squealed, breathless. "Do you love it?"

He pivoted back to her picture of Digger and a big red barn. "I do. I love it more than life itself."

She squeezed him tighter, giggling. "Where's Jessie? Wade?"

"Your sister is working. Wade had to pick up a prize bull out of Denver. He should be back tomorrow."

"Oh!" Her eyelids splayed wide. She pushed her palms against his chest and cast a glance over her shoulder. "Miss Gilmore, come here."

Clancy's heart skipped a beat, and then pounded with a staccato rhythm. He raised his gaze to meet the startled one of his next-door neighbor. Nervous perspiration budded on his forehead. *Damn.* Even his palms felt clammy.

"Mr. Wiseman," she said weakly.

"Miss Gilmore," he grunted, wishing he'd simply have nodded.

Shelby's eyebrows rose as her big blue eyes focused on him, and then on Tess. "You two know each other?" The seven-year-old was too perceptive for her own good. "You do," she breathed.

"Miss Gilmore and I are neighbors."

"Really?" A mischievous grin spread across Shelby's petite face as she began to wiggle out of his arms. "Would it be okay to invite her for dinner? You're gonna feed me, aren't you?" When her feet touched the carpeted floor, she stared up at him. But before he could answer, she spun around and approached Tess. "Clancy is a great cook. Did he tell you that? I bet he didn't."

"Shelby," he growled, feeling his cheeks flush with heat. Yeah. He cooked. It was one of his passions.

Shelby flashed him a *duh* expression. "Well you are." Then she turned her girlish charm on Tess. "So will you come over? Join us? Please, Miss Gilmore? It will be so much fun."

"I— Well— I— Uhm..."

Clancy almost felt sorry for the woman as she stuttered and physically stepped away in an attempt to gracefully back out of the invitation. Evidently she didn't know Shelby. The girl was as stubborn as her sister. With each of Tess's steps, Shelby followed, until she wrapped her arms around the woman's waist.

"*Puhlezzee*," Shelby whined. Those familiar puppy-dog eyes glimmered with a plea that always morphed Clancy into a pile of manageable goo just before he gave her anything she wanted. The girl had him and Wade wrapped right around her little finger.

"She'll do this until she gets her way," Clancy warned. He clamped his lips together to hide his grin. Tess didn't stand a chance against the child. "It's best to give in and go with it." Moving closer, he stopped before them and *ruffled* Shelby's long, ebony hair. As she peered away from Tess, the she-devil winked at him.

Lord, help them.

He hoped she wasn't up to matchmaking, because the boundaries had already been set between him and the schoolteacher. Even if his body heated and his pulse raced with desire every time he got near her, they were not meant to be.

"Join us." He swallowed hard, attempting to keep his voice strong and steady. "Perhaps you can keep the little urchin out of trouble while I tend to cooking."

"Thank you, but I can't. The girls will be home."

"Girls?" Shelby perked up. "Can they come too?"

Tess's mouth parted in what Clancy assumed was another rejection, when he quickly added, "Sure. The more the merrier." Inwardly he groaned. *You're playing with fire.*

"Great!" Shelby slid her hand into her teacher's. "Can I ride with you?"

Tess's jaw dropped as a look of confusion raced across her pretty features. She shook her head and smiled as if she realized that a seven-year-old had just coerced her.

"Uh. Okay." Tess snapped her mouth closed. She did *not* allow a child to lead her right into a predicament she was trying to avoid—spending time with one certain cowboy. But by the gleam in Clancy's eyes, she had done just that.

"I tried to warn you." He chuckled. "How about I take Shelby with me? You can stop by your house and..." he paused before continuing, "and change into something more comfortable." His voice thickened as his gaze slid from her high heels up her bare legs. When his perusal stopped at her hips, his nostrils flared. He quickly raised his sight to meet hers.

For a moment all time stood still. Flashes of their earlier encounter, when he caught her in nothing but her bra and thong, forced a shiver up her spine. Immediately, she broke eye connection, at the same time she released Shelby's hand and took a step backward.

"I— Uh—" She caught herself frowning and eased the tautness from her expression. It was too late to shun the invitation. She would just have to make do. "I'll swing by the house and pick the girls up. Is four thirty okay?"

"That would be great. C'mon, imp." Clancy scooped Shelby up in his arms. "We've got work to do." Snagging Tess's attention again, he trapped her gaze in his heated one.

Then he turned and walked away, leaving her with nothing but the very fine view of his derriere. She continued to stare at his jeans-clad ass until someone stepped up behind her.

"*Oh yeah,*" the woman purred. "Have you ever seen a man who fills out a pair of jeans like that cowboy?"

Tess glanced toward the third-grade teacher she'd met that morning in the office as the woman stopped beside her. Andrea Krueger had to be in her midthirties, but in top-notch condition, right down to her slender thighs.

The tall brunette had yet to take her hungry eyes off of Clancy. "What I wouldn't give to be lost in that man's arms."

Tess's curiosity peeked. "You know Mr. Wiseman?"

"Know him? No." Andrea's mouth turned into an appreciative grin. "But I know about him and his wild reputation." She must have detected Tess's surprise, because a burst of laughter pushed from Andrea's full lips. "You can't tell me you haven't once thought of being spooned between two men, especially one that looks that good."

Without responding, Tess joined Andrea in watching Clancy and Shelby disappear beyond the door.

"No. I haven't," she finally replied.

The woman raised a perfectly plucked eyebrow in disbelief. "Then you must be dead from the waist down." She studied Tess for longer than what was comfortable, before speaking again. "C'mon. Wouldn't you want to experience two strong men cherishing your body?"

Oh, hell yes. But Tess had the good sense to keep her mouth shut, while she shook her head.

"Your loss." Andrea sucked her bottom lip between her teeth. "I think I'll catch up with him. See you tomorrow." Without hesitation, she skirted down the hall.

An ache in Tess's cheeks made her realize she'd locked her jaws together and her face was flush with heat. Just seeing the woman hot on Clancy's heels had brought out the green-eyed monster.

Jealousy?

"Nooo." Tess chuckled, nervously.

Splaying her fingers and then fisting them, she attempted to shake off the tension that had tightened every muscle in her body. Jealousy wasn't possible. She hardly knew the man. But envy? Now that was possible.

Tess inhaled a deep, steady breath. Andrea didn't give a flying fuck about her reputation or what would be said if she hooked up with Clancy. A year ago that would have been Tess, but not now.

She blew out a long, even breath, raising her chin slightly. "Enough," she whispered.

A second ticked by, before she pivoted on the balls of her feet. Quick footsteps carried her back to her classroom. She scanned the room, finding everything in its place, and then she snatched her purse from the desk and left, pulling the door closed behind her.

As she moved down the hall she kept her mind blank. Someone calling her name pulled Tess back to reality. She halted, focusing on what the administrator before her was saying.

Concern burned in Barbara's eyes. "Is everything all right?"

Tess forced a tight smile. "Yes. Of course. Just thinking about tomorrow's schedule."

The woman must have bought Tess's lie, because she cocked her head thoughtfully as her gaze softened.

"Tough being the newbie, but you'll do fine. Go home, put your feet up and have a glass of wine." The abrupt ringing of a cell phone that played a child's ditty snatched Barbara's attention. As she reached for the telephone, she waved good-bye.

Returning the gesture, Tess took that moment to escape. She hurried out of the building and into the half-empty parking lot, noting neither Clancy, Shelby nor Andrea were anywhere in sight.

Climbing into her car, Tess found her thoughts wandering back to one sexy cowboy. She needed a plan, one that would get her through this evening unscathed.

The drive home was uneventful, but as she maneuvered the vehicle down the driveway, she could see Rose and Rachel standing before their destroyed garden. When her sisters heard her approach, they turned, tears shimmering in their eyes.

Braking, she turned off the car, opened the door and got out. "I'm so sorry."

"What happened?" Rose asked.

Rachel sniffled, running a tissue beneath her reddened nose.

Tess cast a quick glance toward the Spanish-style house next door that was visible through tall, willowy trees. "Lightning took down the fence between our properties. One of Wiseman's calves had its way with your vegetables."

"But who did this?" Rachel turned toward the garden.

Following her sister's line of sight, Tess's eyes widened.

Green leafy plants perfectly spaced budded up from neatly groomed rows of rich soil. The memory of Clancy working in the garden as she left this morning rose. It had to have taken money and time to reconstruct the garden. Of course, the plants weren't the mature ones that had once sprouted from the ground. All the same, it must have taken him half the morning, and she was sure he had better things to do than gardening.

"Clancy. I mean Mr. Wiseman," she corrected.

The man's consideration and thoughtfulness had completely thrown her for a loop. Add the loving and caring way he treated Shelby, and Tess was left more perplexed than ever.

"How sweet," Rose cooed, at the same time Rachel released a sappy, "Ahhh..."

Man. Her sisters had it bad for the cowboy. The fact that their neighbor's calf had destroyed their garden didn't seem to matter anymore.

"You'll get to thank him at dinner. He's asked us to join him."

"Dinner!" both girls chimed together as their eyelids widened with pleasant surprise. Huge smiles slipped across their faces.

Tightening the grip on her purse, she pivoted toward their house. "Yes. Just let me change my clothes and we can go—"

"Oh my God. What am I going to wear?" Rachel blurted just before both girls bolted.

Tess had never seen the girls move so quickly as they nearly bowled her over trying to get past her. The screen door creaked open and then slammed shut.

As Tess stepped upon the porch, she released a wary breath.

Which would be worse? Keeping her sisters at arm's length from the charming rogue or keeping her own body from betraying her?

With another sigh of resignation, she entered the house. Without pause she headed toward her bedroom, stopping when she stood before her open closet. What the hell was she going to wear? She chuckled, shaking her head.

"Now I sound like Rachel." Resting her palm upon a small black dress, she growled, "Nah." The silky material had a way of caressing her body, making her feel feminine and sexy.

Metal scraped wood as she pushed one garment after another out of the way. No way did she want to look like she was trying too hard. Then again, she didn't want to look like she wasn't trying, either. Jeans and a soft brown, marble-washed, long-sleeved shirt won out in the end.

After Tess dressed, she exited her room and stepped into the living room only to come face-to-face with Levi. She hadn't expected him home until later that evening. Arms crossed over his broad chest, he scowled beneath his black Stetson pulled low over his eyes.

"What's this about dinner at Wiseman's?"

Eeek! She was not in the mood to be questioned or reprimanded for accepting an innocent dinner invitation or what she hoped to be nothing more than—

"I believe it's called southern hospitality." Before he could respond, she interjected, "Did you know anything about Mr. Peterson purchasing a prize bull out of Denver, Colorado?" His intense expression said she'd successfully managed to change the subject.

Levi unfolded his arms and tipped his hat back with a knuckle. "He must have attended the National Western Stock Show. They're having a huge Angus bull sale in Denver. Did you hear when Peterson was returning?"

She suppressed a small smile. "I think tomorrow."

"Tomorrow..." His hum turned into a spark of excitement. "Well, we shouldn't keep our neighbor waiting. Rose! Rachel! Let's go."

Releasing a heavy sigh, Tess felt the tension riding her shoulders and neck relax. Tonight would be just another night.

Yeah. Right, her subconscious hummed.

Chapter Five

Chopped rosemary, thyme, basil and garlic simmered in a thick tomato paste above a flickering blue flame. On the stainless stove beside the aromatic sauce sat a large, oven-proof skillet. Clancy adjusted the fire beneath the browning cutlets, startling when the doorbell chimed. As he dropped the spaghetti into the boiling water, his pulse began to race and his heart did a little flip-flop. The woman who had consumed his thoughts was here.

The sound of Shelby's rapid footsteps echoed across the Mexican-tiled floor in the living room. "I'll get it."

Since they left the school, she had talked excessively about her new teacher, while his mind had whirled with having Tess in his home—on his turf. Why it meant so much to him, he had no idea. It's not like other women hadn't entered his domain, but for some odd reason it felt different, and he didn't like it one iota.

Clancy rolled his head from shoulder to shoulder in an attempt to halt the building tension. The act of stretching released a series of popping muscles, but did nothing to ease the unwanted stress that lingered.

After Shelby learned Tess's sisters were teenagers, she had been disappointed, but it hadn't dampened her excitement that she would see her new teacher again. Judging by the way Clancy's palms grew clammy, he felt the same way.

Snatching a towel off the counter, he quickly wiped his hands and tossed the cloth over his shoulder, before he headed toward the arched entrance that lead into the living room.

What would she think of his house? Would she enjoy his veal parmesan? Maybe he should have cooked steaks.

"What the hell's wrong with you?" he muttered beneath his breath.

Even as he berated himself for his behavior, he couldn't stop his hand from slipping beyond the waistband of his jeans, ensuring his freshly donned burgundy twill shirt was neatly tucked in. *Damn.* He wished he'd thought of wearing his Stetson. The stupid thought garnered an uneasy chuckle that immediately died when he set eyes on his next-door neighbor.

Dressed in a pair of jeans that hugged her slim figure like a second skin, she glanced quickly around the room until their eyes met. Neither spoke as he slowly approached, although Shelby's chatter never ceased. Caught within the woman's web of enchantment, he didn't hear a thing the little girl jabbered on about. All he could think about was drowning in the bluest eyes he had ever seen, until a man cleared his throat.

Tess blinked, breaking their connection. "Oh. Uh. I'd like to introduce my brother. Levi this is Mr. Wiseman."

He jutted his hand out to the strapping young fellow standing protectively beside his sister. "Clancy."

The boy's glare slid thoroughly over Clancy, head to toe, before he joined his hand with Clancy's. "It's a pleasure to meet you, Mr. Wiseman."

Rose rolled her eyes. "Here we go again." Rachel elbowed her twin in the side. "I'm just saying—" Rose was cut short when all the Gilmore siblings nailed her with a joined scowl.

Clancy grinned. "Hey, Rose. Rachel."

"Hi, Clancy," the girls chimed in unison.

"Your home is beautiful," Rachel cooed in awe. A dreamy expression overtook her as she scanned the rustic room, complete with large, brown leather furniture, western artwork and pine columns.

Rose knelt down, a finger tracing a miniature horseshoe embedded into a three-by-three patch of grout that broke up the light burnt-orange Mexican tile flowing from one room to the next.

"These are adorable." She gazed up at him with large doe eyes.

So young and innocent, something he had never been.

"Can't take all the credit. Shelby's sister helped with the decorating." He glanced at the child who was the spittin' image of Jessie. "Make our guests comfortable, get them a soda from the bar, then set the table, while I check on dinner. I hope you like veal parmesan." His eyes met Tess's again.

Before he turned to leave, Rose sprang up beside her twin. "Do you need help?" they asked as if they were one.

Levi stepped between his sisters and Clancy. "I'll help him." All three of his sisters' jaws dropped at the same time. "What?" he growled. A furrowing frown pulled his eyebrows together.

Clancy could see Tess fighting a smirk.

"Nothing," she choked, while the girls weren't as discreet and giggled.

"Then it's settled. You girls enjoy yourself. Levi, it looks like it's just you and me."

The strapping boy followed, looking about at ease in the kitchen as a long-tailed cat in a room full of rocking chairs. Clancy struggled not to chuckle, but his respect for the young man moved up a notch. He was protecting his sisters from the big bad wolf who lived next door.

Levi pushed his hands into his pockets. His shoulders rose, revealing his first sign of insecurity. "Uh. What would you like me to do?"

"I pretty much have things handled here." Clancy forked a cutlet and then another, setting them in a baking pan, before pouring the tomato sauce and sprinkling a generous portion of mozzarella atop them and placing them in the oven. "Why don't you pull up a seat and tell me about your plans for your ranch."

Relief filtered across the boy's face as he eased his palms from his pockets and took a seat at the large pine table. "I want to build my herd like yours and the Petersons'." He glanced at the bowl of salad and bread sitting before him.

Clancy released a low whistle. "That's quite an endeavor. You have what—about seven hundred acres?" Ribbons of steam curled off the pot of boiling water. Capturing a noodle with a spoon, Clancy tested its firmness. "Even though hill country is a beautiful location to live, the cattle ratio to acre is lower than other parts of Texas. It's a trade off, Levi." Using two potholders, he extracted the pot from the stove and walked toward the sink where a strainer awaited. As he strained the spaghetti, he spoke. "Most of us who run large ranches and live here also supplement our feed by owning separate farming operations in other areas known for their rich soil, production capabilities and cost of land. My land is in hay and wheat."

"Really?" Tess's smoky voice turned both Clancy's and Levi's heads around. Her eyes burned with an intensity that made Clancy's pulse race. "So we can't accomplish what you want to do?" She directed her question to her brother.

"I...well..." Levi stumbled for words, as his face began to flame with color.

"As Levi knows, there's a lot you can do with seven hundred acres." Clancy rushed in to help the floundering young man, while he placed the noodles on a large platter.

"So how many head of cattle can you raise on seven hundred acres?" This time she turned, making it clear her inquiry was meant for Clancy.

"You're looking at six-hundred pounds of live weight per acre. Any more and you'll need to supplement feed." Judging by the way her pretty features tightened, her mind was going a mile a minute. "So we would have to buy or raise additional feed—"

"Looks like it's time to eat." Levi jumped up from the table. "What can I do to help?" Tess narrowed her steely gaze on him. Even though he had stifled his sister's curiosity for the moment, frustration thinned his lips.

Clancy had no doubt this conversation would continue later between the siblings, but for now the boy needed his help. "Tess, how about you grab the salad. Levi if you get the bread, butter and grated cheese, I'll follow you with the main course."

A light glimmered in the dark depths of her eyes, but she remained silent. Instead, she retrieved the large bowl of antipasto salad and turned to leave. Levi heaved the large cutting board with Italian bread on the slab onto one arm, before he gathered the remaining items.

"Something tells me this isn't over," he whispered. As he watched the swagger leave the browbeaten young man as he followed his sister out of the kitchen, Clancy smiled.

No. Tess Gilmore wasn't the type of woman who left things unspoken. He liked that in a woman. It meant he'd always know where he stood with her. Not that he expected their relationship to evolve into anything more than friends— neighbors. Still he had to admit there was something about her that called to him on a different level. Or maybe, it was that he wanted someone he couldn't have.

"Yeah. That must be it," he muttered to himself.

Candles flickered against the subtle lighting in the dining room. Rose and Rachel stood beside a large oak table. Next to them Shelby grinned ear to ear, mischief glimmering in her eyes. Yet Tess knew the warm, sensual ambience had her sisters' special touch tattooed all over it. Thankfully, Clancy had maintained proper decorum with the two impertinent teenagers, not encouraging their childish crushes. Later tonight she'd have a talk with both of them.

As she placed the salad in the middle of the lace-covered table, she had to admit it was beautiful. "Girls, you have outdone yourselves."

Crystal stemware twinkled beneath the lights, while elegant china and polished silverware adorned each place setting. She picked up a delicate, gold-trimmed plate with a spectacular, multicolor scroll design around the rim, interspersed with scenes of two colorful ming birds. The center design showcased an exotic flowering tree and flitting butterflies.

"Oriental?" Tess didn't realize she'd spoken aloud, until Clancy said, "It was my mother's." He glanced toward the china hutch against the wall where matching pieces were arranged, as his voice softened. "She enjoyed all things oriental."

Tess didn't miss the hint of sadness, not only in his words, but also in his expression when their gazes met. Forcing a smile that didn't reach his eyes, he eased out her chair, the legs scrapping against the tile.

The warmth of his fingers whispered across her shoulder as she sat, sending a shiver through her.

"Would you care for wine?"

For a moment, she couldn't respond. She swallowed hard, fighting the flutters in her stomach, knowing she needed to gain her control back and soon.

"Yes. Please," she finally managed to utter, as she heard the others take their seats.

As he moved toward an antique wine cart with mirrored top, she grabbed her napkin, snapping and unfolding it, before she laid it gently in her lap. One, to keep her mind occupied. And two, to steady her trembling hands.

Sheesh. What was it about this cowboy that tongue-tied her and made her body long for his touch?

When Tess decided it was simply because she hadn't been with a man in some time, it was too late. Four pairs of curious eyes were pinned on her. Heat flared across her cheeks. She shot an anxious glance in Clancy's direction only to find the scoundrel unsuccessfully stifling a smile of amusement.

Damn, the man.

"So how was school today?" tumbled from her mouth. When no one answered, she quickly added, "Rose, did you get your math class changed?"

"Yes." Her sister's eyes twinkled.

"Rachel—"

"Yes, Tess, I turned my request in too."

When Clancy moved toward Tess, so close his spicy cologne wrapped around her like a blanket, she completely forgot to ask about the girls' schoolwork. Instead, she gazed into his eyes and inadvertently leaned into him, but quickly righted herself.

He laid a warm hand on her shoulder. "Wine?"

"Wine?" She eased back. "Yes. Please."

The space between them felt charged with electricity. It raised the small hairs across her arms. Awoke every one of her nerve endings. She prayed no one noticed as he filled her glass with the lush, red Merlot. A roguish wink revealed he knew exactly what his presence was doing to her, before he stepped back and moved down the table.

Taking a seat across from her at the head of the table, he unfolded his napkin and set it in his lap. "Dig in."

As the food was passed around, an easy camaraderie fell into place. The twins thanked Clancy for setting their garden to right. He, in return, offered to show Levi how to mend a barbed-wire fence.

Slicing a thin piece of veal smothered in cheese and sauce, Tess placed it in her mouth and closed her eyes. "Mmmm. This is delicious." When her eyelids rose, she could have sworn a blush brightened Clancy's face.

"Thank you. When you live on a cattle ranch you have to find all kinds of way to cook beef."

He spoke so matter-of-factly, but there was so much more to what he had prepared. If she didn't know better, Tess would have sworn she was dining at that exquisite Italian restaurant on the Riverwalk downtown. Not to mention, the wine was perfect, enhancing the flavor with each sip she took.

"Jessie says his stuffed beef tenderloin with mushroom gravy is to die for, but I like his macaroni and cheese." Pinching a noodle between her fingers, Shelby let it drop into her mouth.

Clancy shook his head.

"Where did you learn to cook?" Rachel asked.

His gaze dropped to his plate. The veins in his neck protruded. "My mother." Seconds ticked by before he raised his eyes and reached for his glass of wine. He took a long drink. "The recipe is from my mother's cookbook."

"Does she live in San Antonio?" Rose asked.

"No." Clancy didn't offer more.

Tess was thankful that Rose didn't pursue the subject, because a blind man could see that the issue of his mother was uncomfortable. "So, do you think it would be possible for Levi and me to tour your ranch? Perhaps you could also introduce us to the Petersons. Levi has a million questions and I have more to learn."

Clancy eased back in his chair, clearly relieved for the change in subject. "Tonight?"

"Of course not. Perhaps this weekend, I mean, if it's not inconvenient."

"Saturday would be great. Ty and Wade should be over around eight in the morning. You could kill two birds with one stone."

"I heard the Petersons purchased a new bull out of Denver. Angus?" Levi slipped another bite of veal into his already full mouth.

Clancy slid his gaze from Tess to her brother. "Yes. From his lines it sounds like a good addition to their breeding program."

From that point onward, Levi captured Clancy's attention and their discussion surrounded cattle, land and artificial insemination. Topics that soon bored the girls, except for Tess. She marveled at the cowboy's knowledge. Overwhelmed and slightly disturbed, she wondered if they had bitten off more than they could chew with their ranch.

"I would have prepared a dessert if I'd had the time." Clancy rose and began to stack the plates, while the others followed suit.

"Thank goodness you didn't. I couldn't eat another bite." Shamelessly, Tess had eaten everything on her plate, but it had been so good.

He glanced at Shelby and winked. "I do have homemade ice cream and fresh strawberries."

"Ice cream!" Shelby chirped.

With a nod toward the kitchen, he said, "Go on."

She didn't need encouragement. Shelby was off her feet in seconds and disappeared into the kitchen. When Tess entered, Shelby already had several bowls atop the table and her hand buried deep in a five-gallon tub.

"None for me," Tess said.

After setting the plates on the counter, Clancy opened the empty dishwasher. "It's a nice evening. Why don't you take your bowls on the porch? Tess and I can clean up."

"I'll help," Rose and Rachel chimed together as if they had rehearsed the response.

Tess almost blurted, "What?" The girls hated to do the dishes. As much as she didn't look forward to being alone with Clancy, she thought it better that her starry-eyed sisters keep their distances. "I think we can handle it."

Levi hesitated as if he was considering offering to help, but looked at the baking pan crusted with tomato sauce and cheese and frowned. Cleaning up had never been his favorite either, so Tess wasn't surprised when he picked up his ice cream and followed the girls outside.

Scraping leftover food into the sink, she paused to start the water and flip the switch on the wall. The garbage disposal ground softly, gobbling everything down the drain before she shut it off and reached for a glass.

When she had rinsed the wine from the goblet, she glanced toward Clancy. "Thank you for having us over."

He moved to her side, his shoulder touching hers. "It was our pleasure."

As butterflies flittered in her stomach, she handed him the glass, their fingers brushed. The touch was so innocent, but the power behind it forced their eyes to meet. For a brief moment neither spoke, and then she retrieved another glass. But the casual meeting of their hands, the closeness of their bodies as they stood side by side was more than Tess had bargained for.

This man made her body burn. Every one of her cells sparked with attraction. While her breasts grew heavy, the tingle in her nipples tightened to an almost painful state. And Lord have mercy, between her thighs she felt moist and achy like some horny teenager. It didn't help when he slid his sensual gaze over her. Hell. She could have sworn flames flickered in his eyes.

Needing a break from the sexual tension arcing between them, she stepped away. "I'll gather the kids' bowls." When she pivoted to leave, she could feel his heated stare follow her.

The cool night air was a shock against her flesh. But the carefree laughter she heard warmed her. It had been a while since her sisters and brother had had something to laugh about. She stood for a second listening to Shelby tell about Wade and Clancy's attempts to ride mini-ponies, only to be left in the chute on their butts each time. Just the image of such an impressive man on a pony brought a smile to her face.

"You little rat." The deep baritone voice behind Tess sent a shiver up her back. "That wasn't a story that needed told."

"Oh, Clancy." Shelby jumped up from the porch swing and ran to him, throwing her arms around his waist. "You know it was funny."

He arched a brow. "Not according to my backside." The ringing of his cell phone stole his attention. He reached into his pocket to retrieve the cell and flipped it open to answer it. "Wiseman. Yeah. Sure. Bye." He closed the phone, returning it to his jeans. "Well, you little hellion, it looks like Jessie is heading home."

Just the opportunity Tess had been looking for. "And so are we."

Clancy jerked his attention back to her. "No need to rush. You don't mind hanging out a little longer, do you, Shelby?" he said, without looking at the child.

"Heck no." She beamed up at Levi. When he blushed, Tess fought the urge to chuckle.

"Tomorrow is a school day. The kids have homework, and I need to work on my schedule for tomorrow. Thank you again for dinner." She extended her hand. Clancy's fingers folded around hers and his presence surrounded her, taking her breath away. Shadowed in moonlight he was tall, dark, sexy and way too tempting.

He pulled her closer so their bodies almost touched. Then he leaned in and pressed his lips to her ear. "Are you sure you want to leave?" he murmured.

What a strange question? Of course she was sure, but the warmth of his breath against her skin started her heart hammering. She found herself almost whispering *No*, but choked on the word when Levi moved to her side and Clancy released her.

Stepping away, she watched the cowboy and her family. Tess couldn't help thinking if only it was a different time—a different place.

Chapter Six

Air.

Gasping, Clancy shot upright into a sitting position. Covered in a light sheen of perspiration, he gulped down several breaths. White-hot adrenaline coursed through his veins, feeding his racing pulse as he desperately reached for composure. He'd almost succeeded when he attempted to move his feet and they wouldn't budge.

His heart stuttered, threatening to stop.

As irrational fear gripped him in its tight fist, he kicked his powerful legs and flailed his arms. Only when moonlight sliced through an open window, bringing his surroundings into view, did he begin to cease his struggle.

His bedroom. His home.

The twisted sheets wound around his ankles would have been laughable if not for the shadows that continued to slip in and out of his foggy head. Blinking hard he caught a glimpse of his naked image in a large mirror that hung above his oak dresser across the room.

"Fucking nightmares." It was the same old dream where his mother died at his father's hands.

Exhausted, he plopped backward into the downy softness. But before he could free his legs, more childhood memories rose so quickly he squeezed his eyes closed. A man of twenty-six should be able to admit his mother abandoned him, instead of dreaming that his father had killed her, but bad dreams didn't appear to care about one's age.

The snap of curtains flapping against the brisk breeze filtering through the room carried the clean scent of rain. Moisture began to puddle on the tile. A heavy sigh pushed from his diaphragm. For a moment he thought about getting up and closing the damn thing.

Nahhhh... It could wait a little longer.

Releasing a shuddering breath, he tucked his hands behind his head and the pillow, attempting to relax his body. He sucked in several deep breaths, releasing them slowly. When that didn't work, he rolled over and eased to the edge of the bed, planting his feet on the floor. Cold radiated up his legs going bone-deep. Elbows pressed into his knees, he leaned forward and buried his face in his palms.

He despised dreaming. Most of all he loathed the anxiety that seeped into him on nights like tonight. But this dream had shaken him to the core, because this time he saw his own image in his father's face. Instead of Clancy's mother cringing beneath the man's large hands, he saw Tess.

"Shit."

Clancy pushed to his feet, his fingers splaying wide, before returning them into fists. No way in hell would he become his father, even if it meant never experiencing love or a wife or children—a family.

A picture of Tess sitting at one end of his dining room table across from him while her family laughed at something Shelby said flickered in his mind. Quickly it changed to the moment his and Tess's hands had touched in the kitchen and they gazed deep into each other's eyes. Without a doubt he knew she could fill that something he had longed for in his life, especially since he'd seen how happy Jessie and Wade were together.

Fuck. What was he saying?

He wouldn't know love if it jumped up and bit him on the ass, much less risk putting someone he cared for in the position to live the life he and his mother had. Few in this community knew about his family's history or the dirty little secret that had driven his mother away without a single good-bye.

Hands trembling, he reached for the half-empty bottle on the nightstand. He didn't hesitate tipping the beer to his lips. The moment the warm, bitter ale touched his tongue, he cringed.

"I need a real drink." Even with that said, he downed the rest of the beer, leaving a sour taste in his mouth.

His stomach growled its disapproval, churning a warning to feed it before abusing it more, but Clancy paid it no heed. If he wanted whiskey he would have to get dressed and go out in the stormy night, because he'd finished the last of his good Scotch a couple days ago.

Thunder boomed and a wisp of chilly air reminded him of the incoming weather. He skirted the growing puddle, closing the window a little too hard, causing it to bang and the glass to rattle.

With an exasperated huff, he stabbed his fingers through his hair. Shoulders dropping, he pivoted to stare into the hearth. Embers burned a dying orange-red in the fireplace, giving off the faint scent of pine, but no real warmth.

Once again he scanned the room, locating his jeans draped across an overstuffed chair next to the fireplace. After collecting a clean shirt, skivvies, and socks from his dresser, he collapsed into the chair and tugged his socks on, before he donned his briefs and slipped a T-shirt over his head.

Another heavy sigh pushed from his lips. His hands fell listlessly into his lap. For a moment, he sat unmoving. Tess had haunted his thoughts throughout the week and now that damn dream. Frustrated, he pinched the bridge of his nose, and then he reached for his pants.

The damn things were cold as ice and still damp from the storm he had been caught in earlier while helping Milo feed the stock. As Clancy stuck a leg into his jeans, goose bumps prickled across his skin. The thought of retrieving a dry pair of pants flashed, but what the hell. By the beat of the rain against the bedroom window, he was in for a wet night. Without delay, he finished dressing and pushed to his feet.

Before he fastened his belt, Clancy tucked his shirt into his jeans and paused. *Have I crossed the line—become a drunk like my old man?* Emotion welled. Tears of self-reproach moistened his eyes, but he willed them away with disgust and shame.

Shit. He was tired. Every bone in his body felt weary, knees threatening to buckle. Stumbling, he grasped the chair. "I'm nothing like you."

Not yet, that ominous inner voice whispered.

Truth was he rode a thin line.

Clancy liked to drink and party. Drinking was not only entertaining but a way to drown his loneliness. Still, he'd done without alcohol plenty of times—he just preferred not to.

What needled him the most—got under his skin—was he enjoyed sex a little rough, but not violent like his father. Memories rose fast and furious of his mother's cries, her struggles, ripped clothing, bruises and blood—so much blood.

Again he threaded his fingers through his hair.

Dammit. He'd never lost control with Jessie or any of the other women he had been with. Of course, he usually stuck to one-night stands and threesomes. The second emotions were involved, he hightailed it, because the truth was—he didn't trust himself.

Thoughts of Tess rose again.

Just the way she commanded his attention when she entered a room made his pulse speed, his body tighten. The obvious love she felt for her brother and sisters warmed him, made him yearn to see that look in her eyes when she gazed at him. And the sadness he glimpsed from time to time made him long to hold and protect her. Tell her everything would be okay.

A woman like her could turn him around.

A sudden sense of strength, of purpose, filled him as he crossed the room. He might not be the man for her, but he could be a better man. After tonight, he'd focus more on constructive things. Maybe he'd head down to Austin and check out a couple of horses. He'd been looking to expand his breeding lines. When he pushed open the bedroom door, stubbing his toe against the doorjamb, his resolve faltered.

Who was he kidding? Even if she made him want to be more than what he was—a broken man—they didn't have a shot in hell to be together.

Tess didn't need nor want someone like him, even though he was sure she felt the same magnetic attraction. Hell. The space around them lit up with energy when they came into contact. Still she must have recognized his defect and wisely decided to ignore the impossible draw.

Bad genes.

They were his inheritance. His great-grandfather, grandfather and father had made sure of that. The whole fuckin' male population of Wisemans had been drunks and abusers.

Another earlier memory of Jessie and him speaking about children cut through the thickness of his mind. They had sworn never to marry or bear a child. His dear friend had reneged on one of their promises. How long would it be before she and Wade were setting up a nursery? Unexpected regret rose so swiftly it made him stagger. It took him a moment before he continued.

As he crossed the living room, he stopped at the credenza and scooped his keys, wallet and cell phone off the table against the wall and pushed the items deep into a pocket. Taking a few more steps, he leaned down and retrieved his boots. When the last shoe was on, he grabbed his black Stetson and leather jacket from the hat rack and opened the door, closing it behind him.

No stars riddled the sky filled with heavy gray clouds. The evening's rain had finally turned into a fine mist. A gentle wind caressed his face as he squared his Stetson atop his head and slipped on his coat. Filling his lungs with the moist air, he allowed the clean scent to clear his head, chasing away some of the anxiety that tightened the tendons along his shoulders.

One drink was all he needed, and then he'd go back home and try to get some much-needed sleep. He had plenty to do tomorrow.

On determined footsteps he headed toward his truck and climbed in. For a moment he sat staring into the darkness, knowing he should return to the house and try to get some sleep. Instead, he jabbed the key into the ignition and the engine roared to life.

Tires squealed against the wet asphalt, the empty truck bed fishtailed, side to side. As he maneuvered the vehicle around the circle driveway, he glanced in the rearview mirror at his Spanish-style ranch house that held more haunting memories than good ones—secrets better left buried. He attempted to vanquish his thoughts. Besides, it hurt to think. His temples throbbed with the onset of a headache.

Country music played softly on his radio. The dark stretch of road ahead of him seemed to go on forever. His destination was unknown. How long he drove he didn't know, didn't care. Tonight any ol' watering hole would suffice.

Lights of an oncoming vehicle almost blinded him. Instinctively, his eyelids closed. When he opened them, the neon sign of Fast Freddie's beamed ahead.

"This place will do," he muttered.

The bar was packed for a Thursday night. The parking lot was filled with trucks, jeeps, and an assortment of cars. Several cowboys stood outside the joint while others mingled around a jacked-up pickup sipping on longnecks. A couple of women huddled beneath the awning just outside the entrance, puffing on their cigarettes.

Clancy steered his truck next to a little, red Jaguar and cut the engine. When he opened the door and got out, laughter and loud music assailed him, threatening to drown out his thoughts—just what he needed.

Gravel popped beneath his boots as he headed for the large, double doors. Nodding toward one of the Mendez brothers, cattle ranchers out of Leon Valley, Clancy continued onward while at the same time he reached for his wallet and extracted a ten. A large, burly bouncer accepted Clancy's cover charge and he stepped into the bar, making a beeline for the only thing that calmed his nerves on an evening like this.

Whiskey.

Perhaps it was the fact it was ladies' night, or maybe it was the three-dollar beers advertised, but damn there were a lot of women sashaying around. Clancy took a moment to inhale the scenery, and then realized he was looking for Tess's face in each of the ladies who passed by him.

Uneasy with what he'd discovered, Clancy bellied up to the bar. "A shot of your best whiskey."

The pretty blonde behind the counter flashed him a pearly grin. "Thirsty, cowboy?" She reached beneath the bar and retrieved a dusty bottle. The more dust on the bottle the higher the cost, but who cared.

"Yes, ma'am."

Hip against the counter, he gazed across the crowd. It looked like everyone was having fun, everyone but him. When the bartender set the shot glass of dark mahogany alcohol down in front of him, he tipped his hat.

"Thanks."

Several tears of the liquor fell slowly down the outside of the glass as he reached for the drink and held it to his nose. The consistency was thick, the scent strong and smoky—a sign of quality.

Already he was feeling better. He raised the glass before him in a salute. "Anything worth doing is worth doing right." The wise saying even pertained to getting drunk, in his book.

Without a second thought he tipped the drink to his lips. The smooth burn felt good going down his parched throat—too good. He slammed the glass down with a thud. "Hit me with another and start a tab."

So much for only one drink.

A hearty slap on the back nearly made him spill his next drink. He glanced around to be greeted with a huge grin.

"This is a surprise." Ty eased next to him, signaling the bartender for another cold one. She popped the top on the longneck and it hissed. "Thought you said you were hitting the hay early?" He accepted the beer and took a long swig.

"Changed my mind," Clancy grumbled. Even though his friend was entertaining, he still wasn't looking for company tonight. No, tonight all he wanted to do was forget.

Ty pivoted and leaned so he abutted the counter. Eyeing the crowd, he smiled and tipped his hat when a woman passed by. "Lot of lookers here tonight."

But Clancy wasn't interested. He didn't even turn around, until he heard a scuffle and voices rise. "Well, shit," he groaned. This wasn't good, not good at all.

In the center of the room Tess's brother stood nose to nose with Raúl Mendez. The large man outweighed the boy by fifty pounds. Not to mention, his other three brothers were shuffling through the crowd quickly.

Clancy moved without thinking. In seconds he was by Levi's side.

Laughing, he threw an arm around the young man's shoulders. "Gilmore, where the hell did you run off to?" He attempted to subtly guide the boy out of harm's way, but Levi's expression hardened as he jerked away.

Ty sauntered up beside Clancy. With an upward nod he greeted Raúl. "Mendez."

"This young pup with you?" The Hispanic man threw Levi a scowl.

Ty glanced quickly toward Clancy and then back to Raúl. "Us. He's with me and Wiseman."

Anxiety and excitement crawled beneath Clancy's skin. Kicking someone's ass tonight sounded mighty tempting. Four against three didn't usually concern him, but then again Levi was only a kid. He didn't stand a chance in a brawl with the Mendezes. Nor did fighting ever solve anything or was it likely to set a positive example for the boy. Still the thought of blowing off some steam made his blood simmer.

"Whatever the misunderstanding, it's over," Clancy stated firmly.

"But—"

"Gilmore," Clancy growled, narrowing his eyes on the boy. "It's over. Now shake the man's hand and let's get out of here."

Levi reluctantly extended his hand to Raúl. The handshake might not have been a good idea, because it gave the two angry men a moment longer to glare into each other's eyes. But thankfully Raúl's brothers weren't in a fighting mood. They sandwiched their brother and eased him away, as Ty and Clancy did the same to Levi.

When they were well out the front door, Clancy turned to Levi. "What the hell are you doing in a place like this?"

"What's it to you?" Levi slurred. Swaying away from Clancy, he made a beeline to his truck.

Clancy grabbed him by an arm. "Oh no you don't." When Levi took a swing at him, he ducked, wrapping him in a big bear hug and pinning his arms to his side.

The boy hissed and spit, struggling. All the while Ty leaned against a pickup. Judging by his grin, he was amused. When Levi's energy subsided, he breathed heavily, the scent of too much beer cloaking him.

"Your sister is going to be pissed." Clancy could just imagine the fit she would have when Levi waltzed into the house shitfaced.

"So you're Levi Gilmore?" Ty frowned, taking the boy's measure.

"We've met?" Levi asked.

Ty's chin dipped. "No, but my sister has mentioned you."

Oh shit. Tori Peterson would be right around Levi's age and go to the same school.

"Levi, this is Ty Peterson."

"Ty Peterson?" Levi's eyes widened. "Your sister is fuckin' hot."

Clancy rolled his eyes skyward. The kid had shit for brains.

As Ty moved ominously toward them, Clancy held out a hand, stopping him. "Give him some slack. The boy's drunk. I'll take him home. Can you drive his truck, and then I'll bring you back for yours?" Before Ty could answer, Clancy continued. "Levi, your keys."

"I can drive," he insisted.

"Keys. *Now!*"

The boy dug into his pockets and held out his keys. Clancy grabbed them, tossing them to Ty. That's when Levi stumbled and Clancy caught him.

"Thanks, man. Uh. Anyway, we could do this without my sister getting wind of it?"

Guiding him to his truck, Clancy opened the door. "You're under age and you're drunk. As I see it you have two choices. Either you tell her or I will."

Levi climbed in and waited until Clancy was behind the wheel before he collapsed, his body going limp as his head struck the window with a bang.

"Levi?"

The boy didn't answer.

Clancy chuckled. "Boy, I wouldn't want to be you come tomorrow." He started the truck, cramming it into gear for the drive home.

The only good thing about this night was he would be able to see Tess once again.

Chapter Seven

Dressed in her flannel pajamas, Tess paced the floor one more time. Where the hell was Levi? She had called Johnny's house only to discover her brother wasn't there. Her second telephone call to another friend resulted in no answer, which was the same with Levi's cell phone. He always answered his phone.

Anxiety crawled across her skin, raising goose bumps. It was approaching midnight. Where could he be? She wrapped her arms around herself and made another pass. The roar of an engine and gravel popping in the driveway made her pulse leap. Without hesitating, she ran for the door and flung it wide.

"You are in so much trouble—" Her words died along with the rash of shit she had perched on her tongue. It wasn't Levi's truck that stopped before her, but Clancy's crew-cab. She attempted to peer inside, but the windows were so dark it made it impossible.

When Clancy stepped out of his truck he didn't give her his usual roguish smile. No. Tonight there was something dark in his eyes that even the moonlit night couldn't hide.

Something was wrong. She sensed it.

The air in her chest thickened as he moved toward her. It didn't help that Levi's truck pulled into the driveway and it wasn't her brother behind the wheel.

Tess's feet froze where she stood. "Where's my brother?"

Her heart nearly stopped when Clancy opened the passenger door and her brother spilled into his arms. Her feet found wings as they carried her to Levi's side.

"Oh God. What's wrong?" Then she smelled the strong scent of alcohol. "He's drunk?" Her voice screeched, before heated anger swept across her face. "You did this to him?" She widened her incriminating glare now pinned on Clancy. "I can't believe you'd give a minor alcohol." Her fingers curled into fists. "He's only eighteen." She barely held back the growing need to strike the man. "How could you?"

Look what the bastard had done to her poor brother. Unconscious, Levi's body was limp, smelling like a distillery.

"Now hold your damn horses," someone behind her barked.

Tess whirled around to face the cowboy marching toward her with purpose. Ty came to a halt before her, frowning.

"Clancy saved your brother from getting his lily-white ass kicked, *twice* tonight."

Her brow furrowed. "What?"

"This is none of Clancy's doing," Ty grumbled. "It's that wild-haired brother of yours." The man sounded pissed, but why?

Confused, she shot a glance toward Clancy still holding her brother upright against the truck. "I don't understand."

Ty scowled at her brother. "The little *bastard—*"

"Ty," Clancy growled, stopping his friend cold. Then his voice softened as he turned toward her. "This is probably best discussed between you and Levi."

As Clancy heaved her brother over a shoulder as if he weighed a feather, Tess struggled to withhold a million questions. She followed him silently, every nerve burning with the need to know what had happened. Then the memory of Monday night and the smell of alcohol came to mind. She'd thought it was the beer she had partaken in. Now she wasn't sure.

Oh God. How long had he been drinking? Had she been so wrapped up with starting a new job, getting things organized around the house, she had missed all the signs?

Thoughts of her parents' death, the car accident, sent a shiver through her. What would have happened if he had gotten behind the wheel? Tess couldn't bear losing another family member. Tears sprang from out of nowhere, but she wiped them away before she entered the house behind all three men.

Moving quickly through the room, she said, "Lay him on the couch."

When Clancy eased her brother down, his head thudding against the arm of the sofa, she knelt before Levi's listless body. His lips were parted. He snored softly. The need to touch him, make sure he was okay, was too powerful to dismiss. She reached out and stroked his cheek, feeling stubble beneath her fingertips. His cheeks were cold, but warmth lay beneath. Thank God, he was alive. She released a pent-up breath, thinking *at least for the moment.*

Because tomorrow she was going to kill him.

Worrying her bottom lip with her teeth, she couldn't help wondering what had he been thinking? Didn't he realize their survival depended upon all of them pulling together? If something had happened to him—

A hand settled on her shoulder, startling her. She looked up to see Clancy hovering over her. He gazed down at her with sympathy in his eyes.

"Don't be too hard on him. He only did what boys do."

Tess didn't respond. She returned her attention to her sleeping brother. Crescent eyelashes against his cheeks, his firm jaw, chin so like their father's. Didn't he know they didn't have the luxury of being like other people? They were different. Their lives were different. She and her siblings were all they had. No family. No backup plan. Nothing, except for each other.

When she heard the door close quietly, she realized that Ty and Clancy had left. Pushing to her feet, she stood and began to tug one of Levi's boots off, and then the other. After retrieving the throw over the back of the couch, she laid it over him, tucking the ends beneath him before she gently pushed a sofa pillow beneath his head.

"Tess." He stirred, his eyelids rising halfway to reveal bloodshot eyes. "S-sorry. Wiseman—" His eyelids drifted down. "D-don't blame him." And then her brother passed out again.

Shame and regret flooded over her in waves. He was right. The outcome could have been disastrous, if not for Clancy. She could have lost—

Pinching her lips together, she beat back rising tears. When she found her control, she released another heavy breath.

Instead of thanking Clancy, she had accused and condemned him. He hadn't even attempted to defend himself. Had he realized she didn't want to believe Levi would do anything so careless? Needed someone to blame this on? Because without being able to shun the responsibility she would have to face the truth.

She sucked as a guardian and a sister.

Tess turned her eyes toward the ceiling. "Mom. Dad. I can't do this." Batting her moist eyelashes, she hissed. "Dammit. I won't cry." Crying never got her anywhere. It couldn't change the past and it wouldn't make this situation better.

Hugging herself, she started to pace. *Why?* kept pushing its way into her mind, but no answer clambered to the surface.

Pausing, she glanced at her brother. She had given Levi a lot of leeway. He needed to feel some sense of control after what had happened to their parents. They all did. But she'd made a mistake—a big one. Levi needed a stronger hand, a man to guide him.

Thoughts of Clancy—his silent strength—made her start walking again. She still didn't have any idea what had happened tonight. Maybe her neighbor could shed some light. Maybe he could suggest how she should address the issue. One thing she did know was that she had to know more before confronting Levi tomorrow. With that in mind, she hightailed it to her bedroom.

It didn't take her long to don a pair of underwear and bra, jeans, T-shirt, and slip her feet into flip-flops. Within seconds she was dressed and headed into the hallway and through the house.

Checking Levi once more, she found him curled on a side, sleeping like a baby. Doubting the boy would wake any time soon, she made a beeline to the door and grabbed her keys off the wall unit before she let herself out.

A cold breeze nibbled at her nose and stroked her hair like a lover's caress. She'd left in such a hurry she'd forgotten her jacket. Before she lost her courage, she climbed inside her car and started the engine. In seconds she was pulling out of her driveway and heading down the road.

As she grew closer to her destination, she spied a single light burning bright through the window of Clancy's house. For a brief moment, she slowed the car and thought about turning around. Instead, she accelerated.

Tess needed answers.

Her determination stayed its course, even as she maneuvered the car into the driveway and pulled it to a halt. Still running on resolve, she stepped out of the vehicle. Above her a light sprinkle began. The misty rain hastened her steps down the sidewalk. When she came to the door, she sucked in a deep breath and raised her fisted hand. Before she could knock the door swung open.

Clancy glanced over her shoulder, quickly scanning the area, before he met her gaze. "Is everything all right?"

"Yes. No. I mean— I need to know everything that happened tonight. Why was Levi drinking? Did something happen? And what about these fights?" She shivered as a large raindrop plopped on her forehead, followed by another.

Widening the door, he took a step backward. "Come inside before you get soaked."

After she entered, he closed door, and then surprised her by pulling her into his warm embrace. "Where the hell is your coat?"

Instead of answering, she found herself snuggling closer, his heat a magnet she couldn't resist. "I need answers."

Damn. He smelled good. Earthy. Masculine.

He brushed a hair out of her eyes. "Darlin', you'll have to ask your brother."

"But Ty said you saved him from getting his ass kicked, *twice.*"

There was something odd to his uneasy chuckle, but it became all too clear when he spoke again. "One of those times was from Ty. It appears his sister has caught your brother's eye."

"Oh Lord." Tess dropped her shoulders in despair. "Drinking *and* girls?"

"A man's two worse vices." Clancy laughed, but quieted when she bit her bottom lip, looking so lost, so crestfallen.

"I don't know what to do," she whispered, more to herself than to him. Then she looked up at him with watery eyes and a forlorn expression that nearly broke his heart. "I can't do this."

Damn Levi.

Clancy tightened his hold on her, wanting, no, needing to make everything all right. "Everything will be okay." In fact, he'd kill the little bastard himself if he ever did this to Tess again.

"Okay?" she choked on the word. "How? I don't know how to raise a child, much less three precocious teenagers. Rose and Rachel need a mother to guide them. Levi needs a father." She shuddered, rattling on without taking a breath. "Then there's the fact I don't know anything about cattle or—or horses. I can't run a ranch now, much less when Levi leaves for college. And then there's that." This time she sucked in a big gulp of air, releasing a weary utterance when she exhaled. "He doesn't want to go to college. He wants to be a cowboy—a rancher. Oh God," she said breathlessly. "I've placed my entire family in a lose-lose situation. This is my fault. If I fail—"

"No, Tess," he said firmly. "You won't fail. Darlin', everything you've done is out of love. No one can fault you for that."

A half laugh-half cry pushed from between her thinned lips. "No? The law says I'm responsible. I'm their guardian. Do you know what the judge will say when he sees that I've purchased a ranch that we won't even be able to raise cattle on?"

"Now, I didn't say you couldn't raise cattle on this land, because you can. I just said that—"

A tear slid down her cheek, followed by another. Her bottom lip trembled.

Clancy wiped at her emotion with a knuckle. "Please, baby, don't cry." But just saying the words seemed to open the floodgates.

Tess gasped, releasing a whimper that nearly crushed him.

"I can't do this." She gulped down a mouthful of air. "I've been so wrong. Moving. This ranch. And you." She rambled on. "I'm sorry. So sorry. I know you had nothing to do with Levi's drinking tonight. But—"

"Shhh, baby. It's all right." His lips lightly touched hers. "Everything will be okay."

She shook her head as if she couldn't accept his words.

Her tattered emotions tightened like a hangman's noose around his neck. His gut clenched. Like most men, he didn't do well with tears. He struggled for a moment on what to do—to say. Then he swallowed hard, holding her so near that she buried her face into his shoulder. Her fingers were tangled in the back of his shirt as she held on and wept.

Ty entered the room quietly. He stood silently, watching. The helplessness in his friend's expression pretty much summed up exactly how Clancy felt.

Rubbing his cheek against Tess's, he murmured, "Shhh, darlin'." Each convulsive gasp that shook her was like claws ripping at his heart.

Tess was right. Everything wouldn't magically be all right and it had been wrong to infer it. But, dammit, if there were anything he could do to make it easier for this woman, he'd do it.

"Please, darlin'." He rocked her softly. "We'll make this better, together."

Ty's eyes widened at his impulsive promise.

Yeah. Clancy knew he was treading on dangerous ground, but what could he do? She was a woman in need, not to mention she lived next door. It wouldn't be neighborly to let her flounder, especially when he could do something to help. The problem was accomplishing this without getting involved. That would be the tricky part.

When Ty nodded toward the door as if he planned to leave, Clancy shook his head. The last thing he needed was to be alone with Tess when both their guards were down. Not with how perfect she felt in his arms. The way their bodies aligned as if they were two parts of a whole.

She hiccupped several times, her sobs quieter, starting to diminish.

When he brushed his hand down her long, golden hair, she raised her tear-stained face, placing their lips a whisper apart. Warm, peppermint breath spread across his skin. He didn't know who made the first move, but he felt the quake that rushed through her into him when their mouths met.

Clancy swallowed her next cry, but this one was different. It didn't hold her previous pain. No. This one was of hunger—a need too overpowering to refuse as she deepened their kiss.

For a moment, he felt like the doors of heaven opened up and he tumbled inside. But when her small hand slipped beneath his T-shirt, stroking up his back, it was his turn to tremble, awakening his body with a jolt. Tingles started at the base of his cock and spread outward, every nerve ending going on full alert.

As her tongue swept along his, he tasted her desire, sweet and feminine. He speared his fingers through her hair. Tightening his hold to guide her head back, he broke their caress, before pressing his lips against the silky skin of her arched neck.

Her desperate mewl coaxed a rumble deep in his throat. Everything inside him screamed he had to have this woman. Only when a firm palm came down on his shoulder did he remember Ty's presence.

"Mmmm. Wouldn't mind some of that sugar." His eyes shimmered with lust.

Clancy glanced questioningly at Tess. Her chest rose and fell swiftly. Her nostrils flared, before she reached out and pulled Ty close.

When their sultry kiss ended, Ty smiled. "She's like summer rain on the tongue, isn't she?" Brushing her hair aside, he nuzzled her neck. "Her skin is like silk."

The man was right.

Tess did taste of summer rain, of a day bursting with promise, of life and a future. The image of Clancy and her sitting on the back porch in the swing, cuddled together, while the heavens spilled from above them washed over him.

For the first time tonight he relaxed. With Ty there, Clancy could be close to her with no fear of hurting her. He could do all the things he had dreamt of doing with her.

Before he realized it, he murmured, "I need you," against her lips, and then he froze. *Want. Not need.* But it was too late to take back the Freudian slip.

Chapter Eight

Oh. My. God.

Tess stood speechless, sandwiched between two men. While Clancy stared longingly into her eyes, his lips a mere breath from hers, Ty's firm chest and an impressive hard-on pressed to her back. His hands, which had been moving from her waist to her hips, stilled when Clancy spoke.

I need you.

The cowboy had no idea of the real meaning of *need*.

Talk to a woman who had been celibate for the last year. Her breasts felt heavy, sensitive. A throbbing pulse beat between her moist thighs. And her insides were a furnace of excitement just thinking of making love to not one, but two men—at once.

While her body screamed with joy, her mind whirled. She'd love nothing more than to get naked with these cowboys, fulfill the itch that she'd experienced ever since she met her next-door neighbor, but she didn't dare. Did she?

"That makes two of us," Ty whispered against her ear, sending a chill up her spine.

"Whad'ya say, darlin'?" Fire burned bright in Clancy's eyes. "Wanna take these ol' cowboys for a ride?"

Oh Lord, she must be dreaming.

Clancy shifted a leg and she felt his arousal, hard and thick, against her abdomen. When he traced his nose along hers, their lips touched in the process.

"Please," she moaned, leaning in for a kiss that was withheld when Clancy eased back.

"Please, what?" The gravelly texture of his voice made her heart pound faster.

She flexed her fingers in an attempt to not pull him closer. "Tell me to go home." She made a desperate plea—one that would save her from making the biggest mistake of her life. "Make me leave."

"Do you want to leave?" He gazed through sexy, hooded eyes showing an array of emotions. Desire. Tenderness. And if she didn't know better, possessiveness.

Confused and thrilled, she startled, tensing, when Ty's warm, wet tongue circled the shell of her ear. But the rogue didn't stop there. He licked a slow path down and up her neck, stopping to nibble and suck on her earlobe.

"Are you sure you want this? Me? Ty?" Something felt off in his tone when he said the other man's name, but she ignored it. Instead, Tess fought to keep her wits about her.

If she were wise, she'd get the hell out while the getting was good. Uncertainty made her hesitate, but then Clancy pressed his lips to hers and every rational thought fled. She literally melted against him. As he made love to her mouth, Ty stroked the sensitive skin between her shoulder and neck, his short-cropped mustache and beard tickling her. Moving restlessly between them, she softly moaned.

"Yes." Her breathy hiss appeared to surprise all three of them, because both Clancy and Ty stopped what they were doing.

Tess wanted what they offered. Damn the consequences. Tomorrow she'd pick up the pieces. But at this moment she needed to feel alive, needed to forget what happened with Levi tonight, forget her responsibilities, and especially the loss of her parents. Right now all she wanted was to be in these two men's arms.

"Too many clothes," Ty complained, plucking at her top.

Tess caressed her gaze from Clancy's chest to his eyes. "Way too many."

He reached for the hem of her shirt. "Then let me suggest we start with this." As he pulled the garment over her head, she heard him suck in a breath. The lacy bra she wore didn't do much to cover her breasts.

Ty moved around her to stand next to Clancy. He made a head-to-toe scan, releasing a low whistle as the corner of his mouth rose into a cocky grin. "Damn, baby. You're beautiful."

Clancy just stared at her. She didn't miss the way his jeans tightened around his hips or the swell of his cock. A cock she had full intentions of feeling deep inside her.

"Now it's your turn." Tess had never been shy in asking for what she wanted. And, Lord knew, she wanted it all.

When neither of them made a move, she reached behind and unfastened her bra. Sides tucked beneath her arms, she controlled the material, not allowing it to slip loose until the exact second she wanted it to. As she eased a strap down one shoulder, the men reacted at once, quickly shunning their shirts.

Now Tess knew she was dreaming.

Two half-dressed, gorgeous men stood before her and they only had eyes for her. In fact, she felt like Little Red Riding Hood surrounded by wolves, and by the gleam in their eyes they had every intention of gobbling her up. A wave of desire released, dampening her thighs with the thought of parting them and one, if not both, men going down on her. She clamped her legs together but it did no good to assuage the throb, especially when she gazed at the bronzed, muscled flesh before her.

Both were handsome, broad-chested and had defined arms cut with muscle, Ty being the larger of the two. But Clancy's darker looks, his deep, rich olive skin, and the way his jet-black hair shined silver-blue in the sun, were more what attracted Tess. From the moment she had set eyes on this man there was something about him that just did it for her.

"Now you." Clancy broke into her wanderings.

Without a second thought, she shrugged her shoulder and let the bra drop to the floor.

"Damn, Wiseman. Where did you find this goddess? She even has a four-pac abdomen." Ty stated, but he wasn't looking at the abdomen that hours working out in their home gym had developed. The man's heated stare was on her breasts. She'd have to remember to call Dr. Watts and thank him for the D implants.

"I guess you could say she stumbled over me."

Tess met the amusement shining in Clancy's eyes and they both laughed. Yes. She had literally fallen over him that night, but more so than she would ever let on to. Tonight was a one-shot event. Tomorrow she would refocus on what she needed to accomplish, but for now all she planned to do was enjoy the moment—the men, especially the cowboy next door.

Clancy didn't think it possible he could get any harder, but he did. Her firm, full breasts demanded he put his face between those beautiful full globes, inhale her feminine essence, and just savor the feel of them against his skin. Instead, he silently cursed, struggling to keep his raging hormones in balance. Tightness in his chest and pressure in his head were building, along with a sense of anticipation and anxiety. There was something about this woman that threw him off his game. He had to get his shit together.

"Well, boys. How about removing those belt buckles."

The sensual slide of her voice over his heated skin set his pulse racing. "You first, darlin'." Where he found the strength to dismiss her sexy request he didn't know.

She cocked an elegant brow, eyeing him with interest. This was a woman who was used to getting what she wanted when she wanted. Still she reached for the button of her pants, plucking it free before pausing. Slowly she dragged her zipper down, and Clancy could have sworn he felt the whisper of metal against metal run down his spine.

Was she wearing a thong like she had earlier in the week when he caught her slipping out of her muddy clothes on the back porch of her home?

When she tucked her thumbs into her jeans, dragging them and her panties past her rounded hips, Ty hissed, "Sweet Jesus."

Like Clancy, Ty must have forgotten to breathe when she stood before them stark-ass naked, because he gasped on his next inhale. The woman was a *real* blonde judging by the light curls between her thighs.

Her body was a perfect hourglass of curves. But it was the confidence in her sexuality as she approached them that made it feel like fire raced through his veins. A toothache of a throb pounded in his groin. His palms grew clammy and his pulse beat a staccato.

At that moment he needed this woman more than he needed air. Needed to feel her skin against his, her heart next to his, and her voice whispering she wanted him.

To his surprise, she walked right up to him, her arms going around his neck as her cool flesh met his. As she moved against him, her nipples rubbed erotically over his chest, making his cock swell even more. All his senses began to intensify, sharpen on her.

"Damn, darlin'," was all he could say. Her uninhibited nature intrigued him. How far would she take their lovin'? Would she be up for a little bondage—a little pain?

"Let's play." Ty bent his head and nuzzled his lips down the satiny hollow of her neck.

Her eyes dilated, interest sparking. "Play?" When their gazes met, a feeling of weightlessness came over him, as if he were growing smaller, moving toward those beautiful pools, and he hadn't taken a step.

He shook his head, attempting to regain his composure.

"Not this time." It was too soon. Clancy didn't want to scare her, and there was his growing need for her. He wasn't sure how long he'd last. Just looking at her cheeks, he could feel them against his fingers. Feel her lips pressed against his. *Shit.* If he didn't feel her warm haven surrounding him soon, he might just embarrass himself. Something that had never happened before, but then again, he'd never been with a woman who aroused him to such heights.

Again, she raised an inquisitive brow.

He smoothed a hand up her waist until he held her breast in his palm. "I need to taste you." Pinching the bud, he rolled the taut peak between his fingers. Then he leaned down and latched on.

When his teeth scraped the tender flesh, she tossed back her head, her mouth parting on a cry only to have Ty capture the wispy utterance with a passionate kiss, one that made Clancy's skin draw tight and uncomfortable.

If he didn't know better he'd think he was jealous, but how could he be? He barely knew this woman. Still he wanted to rip her away from the man. The irrational thought fled his mind when he slipped a hand between her thighs, stroked the soft folds of her pussy, before separating the swollen lips and dipping inside.

Ty swallowed another of her cries.

Damn. She was hot, wet and aroused.

Three conditions in a woman that literally made Clancy sing with male satisfaction. As he plunged his middle finger in and out of her heat, his thumb grazed over her clit and began a slow, circular motion. Undulating her hips, she eagerly met each of his thrusts.

"Now—" Her husky voice broke on a breath. "Fuck me, now."

"Well, partner, whad'ya think?" Ty asked.

"I'm not through sampling what you have to offer." Removing his finger from within her, Clancy dropped to his knees, wedging both hands between her legs to drive them farther apart. Then he lowered his head, inhaled her musky scent, before placing a kiss at the heartbeat of her pulse.

"Clancy!" Her knees buckled, but Ty held her upright.

"Mmmm." Clancy blew warm air over her moist flesh and she gasped.

Dragging his tongue along her labia, he felt tiny bumps of hair follicles. His cock twitched angrily against his jeans. The material was too confining and unyielding. Reaching for his zipper, he eased it down. Immediately, his cock pushed beyond the folds.

Long, slow licks across her velvety surface once more elicited another moan from Tess that slid over his flesh like silk. Without another thought he stabbed his tongue into her. Soft skin like taffy folding around him, her inner muscles tightened, drawing him deeper. With each penetrating swipe her light, sweet taste went crazy against his tongue.

Tess's legs began to quiver beneath his palms. She bent her knees, opening herself even more as the shaking intensified. Pressure built, her inner walls contracted in small, jerky motions, discharging a thinner, sweeter fluid that exploded into his mouth.

"Oh God!" she yelped.

Clancy moaned deep into her pussy, sucking and drinking of her essence. He shook his head rapidly as he devoured her. Her scent all over him was provocative and downright hot. With his hands, he cupped her ass, held her immobile as he lapped at her folds, stabbing his tongue inside her again and again. But her thrashing made it difficult to continue. Still an omnipotent rush of power and dominance surged through his veins with the knowledge he had brought her to orgasm so quickly.

When he looked up it was to find her eyes closed and an expression of ecstasy softening her features. As he expected, beneath the proper veneer of a schoolteacher lay a firecracker of a woman.

He got to his feet as Tess's eyelids fluttered opened. Her nose wrinkled as she smiled. "I needed that," she literally purred.

When she reached out to him, fingers circling his biceps, and pulled him forward into her embrace, his heart was pounding so hard he feared it would explode. Her touch was enough to overwhelm his senses, but then their mouths came together in a heated frenzy. She moaned and he lost himself in her arms. Like a parched man, he greedily drank from her lips. Only when Ty cleared his throat did they part.

Clancy and Tess glanced the man's way and burst into laughter. The dumbass cowboy was stark naked except for his Stetson, boots and a big country grin. He'd even donned a condom on his very erect cock.

Wagging his eyebrows playfully, he approached them. "Let's get this rodeo rocking."

As Ty grabbed Tess's hand, the last thing Clancy wanted was to let this beautiful woman go, but he had to. She didn't belong to him and she never would. Whatever silly infatuation he had about her was better left unspoken, because Tess deserved more than a broken man. A wave of melancholy swept over him. He dropped his arms from around her waist and took a step backward, turning away.

Dammit. He had to start thinking of her like every other woman in his life. No ties. No commitments. Just sex. With that thought in his mind he started toeing off his boots. Next he shunned his jeans and skivvies. When he pivoted back around, Ty and Tess were nowhere to be seen.

Laughter spilled down the hall. After rolling his head from side to side, muscles and tendons cracking, he followed the sound that led to his bedroom.

As he pushed the door open and stepped inside, his heart did a flip-flop. Tess lay atop his large knotty-pine bed, her blonde hair a halo surrounding perfect, porcelain features against *his* pillow. Tomorrow her scent would be all over where he laid his head.

She smiled up at him in such a sexy, sensual manner, something clicked inside him. He damn near melted where he stood. Naked and aroused, she appeared exactly how he had imagined her night after night, staring up at him with lustful eyes for only him. The mirage disintegrated in a puff of smoke when Ty crawled upon the bed next to Tess.

Clancy turned away before he even realized what he was doing. Heat raced up his neck, singeing his ears as it spread fast and furious across his cheeks. Irrational jealousy spilled red-hot through his veins.

Dammit. This was turning out harder than he imagined.

Clancy had never thought twice about sharing a woman. He wouldn't start now. His mind was in the right place, but not his consciousness. In an attempt to gather his composure, he strolled over to the flagstone fireplace and picked up a poker, stabbing the cold embers like they were his enemy. When he discovered what he was doing, he leaned over to retrieve a log.

"Cowboy?" Tess chuckled. "I'd rather you start a fire over here than there."

As he straightened up, Clancy fisted his hands, and then he flexed them, trying to relax. When he felt more himself, he slowly faced her. "So, darlin'..." He took a step toward her, forcing a smile he didn't feel. "Just how do you plan to ride these two ol' cowboys?"

Her eyes widened, and for the first time since the three of them had come together he saw her confidence slip. "I...well..." Her brows furrowed.

"Come here, baby." Ty pulled her into his arms. "I think there's too much talking goin' on." He pressed his mouth to hers, while he shot Clancy a *what-the-hell-are-you-thinking* expression.

That was the problem. Clancy was thinking about Tess, about the three of them, way too much. He didn't want to share her, but even as the thought entered his mind, his gaze went to the pair, their lips locked together in a passionate kiss.

Damned, if his cock didn't tighten.

"Well fuck," he silently cursed, before reaching into one of the nightstands next to his bed and retrieving a condom.

Chapter Nine

Even as Ty feverishly kissed her, Tess couldn't help wondering what had happened between the living room and the bedroom. Clancy had given her the best orgasm she had ever experienced, and then he turned cold. Yes. Ty had dragged her away from Clancy as he was undressing, but that shouldn't have—

She gasped, breaking their caress.

Just the sensation of Clancy's warm body brushing against her back set her pulse racing. Then he melded their bodies together as if they were two pieces of a puzzle fitting perfectly together. Tess couldn't help it. She glanced over her shoulder, meeting the most intense stare she had ever witnessed.

"Kiss me," he demanded. The first time he had showed any dominating qualities. Tess had to admit she was enjoying this side of him.

Splaying his strong fingers over her cheeks, holding her to do his bidding, he drew her nearer. In the process she eased upon her back. Halfway draping himself across her, his weight pushed her into the softness of the mattress. His body, skin to skin, felt so good she circled his neck and stretched to eagerly meet him. When their lips touched in a gentle, soulful caress, a shiver slid up her spine. No one had ever kissed her like this.

She wanted this man.

Somewhere between her tears and fears, the strength this man lent had her throwing caution to the wind. Tomorrow she would have to recoup some of her better judgment, but not tonight—not right now. She caught the scent of sandalwood before her, mixing with a hint of citrus aftershave behind her.

Slanting his head, Clancy pushed beyond her lips to deepen the kiss. As his tongue slid along hers, she tasted herself. His essence blending with hers had a heady flavor, one that heated her blood, and one she could get used to if she wasn't careful.

When their lips parted, a wimpy, bereft sound escaped. She should have been embarrassed, but she needed—hungered for—this cowboy. Later she could think of how to put things to right.

"More." She arched into him, loving the erotic abrasion of her nipples against his lightly matted chest.

He ground his teeth together, making a scraping noise. Like fingernails against a chalkboard she felt the harsh sound across her skin as goose bumps rose. For a second she thought his frown meant she'd done something wrong. Doubt flew out the window when his mouth angled over hers once more, but this time there was no gentleness, no tenderness, only a ravenous hunger that matched her own.

When and how it happened, she had no idea. But he was atop her, his hips between her thighs. With one thrust he penetrated her so deep that it robbed her of breath. One after another, he slammed into her relentlessly, each stroke setting her on fire. With their mouths still locked together, her mind started to spin as she found herself rolling, only stopping when she was situated atop him.

"Oh God!" The exclamation burst from her lips in a single breath.

He was so deep inside her the crown of his erection struck the back of her sex. While her heart pounded out of control, he fucked her hard and fast, feasting on her mouth to turn her inside out. Her skin felt too tight, too sensitive. Every nerve ending threatened to explode.

A squeal of surprise erupted from her as a cold substance spread over her anus. *Oh Lord.* She'd completely forgotten Ty was in the room with them. But he was definitely making his presence known as well as his intentions.

Tess tensed, gasping for air. She'd taken it in the backdoor, but never while another man lay beneath her, filling her so sweetly as he mated with her mouth.

"Relax, darlin'. Breathe," Clancy coaxed, slowing his thrusts. He took her bottom lip between his teeth and pulled, forcing her attention before he released his hold. "You'll enjoy this. I promise." He smoothed his callused palms over the cheeks of her ass. "Just focus on me. How my dick fits perfectly inside you." He gripped her rounded globes, easing them apart, making Tess feel exposed and excited.

Then Ty slipped a finger inside.

She groaned, low and long. The sensation of having two men fill her sent chills across her skin.

Clancy raised his hips, meeting the rhythm of Ty's digit. "It's like you were made for me—" He hesitated before adding, "Us."

"Tight," Ty's sandpapery voice growled. Another finger joined the party. He scissored them, stretching and preparing her for something bigger. "You should have seen her come earlier, Wiseman. Damn. She was beautiful." He sucked in a taut breath. "Can't wait any longer."

The mattress sank as he crawled between both her and Clancy's legs. When Tess felt the nudge of Ty's cock against her anus, she couldn't help it—she tensed again.

"Easy, darlin'. Look at me. *Tess.* Look. At. Me," Clancy repeated firmly. Their eyes met. "Now breathe, baby." He inhaled.

She mimicked him, but her arms shook with the energy it took to hold herself above him. When Ty inched farther in, a burning pain erupted at her entrance. She made a sound between a cry and a groan.

"Kiss me," Clancy demanded, again. "Now."

As their mouths touched, Ty eased forward, stretching her wider, carefully pushing deeper. She closed her eyes, trying to block out the discomfort.

"Look at me," Clancy insisted.

Lucky for her Ty breached the second ring of muscles and her eyelids literally flew open, meeting Clancy's intense stare.

"It's over, darlin'." He quietly soothed her. Pressing his lips to hers, he murmured, "It's over. You did great." He planted several light kisses to each corner of her mouth.

"Damn, Clancy." Ty's strained voice whispered against her ear. "She's so tight. So fuckin' hot." His broad chest lay flat against her back, his hips against her ass, sandwiching her between the two of them.

Heavy breathing filled the room, including hers.

It seemed like forever before Ty moved. His strong hands gripped her hips, as he withdrew almost completely out of her body, before he eased back in. Each exquisite stroke was meant to satisfy him as well as her. Their voices joined in a series of moans.

Then Clancy shifted, his hips rising to match Ty's rhythm.

Oh God. Tess knew she'd died and gone to heaven. She didn't have to do anything, just relax and enjoy.

Closing her eyes, she savored their slick bodies gliding in unison. But her repose lasted only a minute. Two cocks pumping in and out began to push her entire system into overload. Thoughts became jumbled. Her body felt as if it were going up in flames. She shook, unable to control what was happening to her, and then she was falling, helplessly falling into the dark abyss.

Stars burst behind her eyelids. The muscles in her belly clenched. Tingles became unyielding contractions that unmercifully squeezed harder and harder until she couldn't breathe, didn't try.

Her orgasm struck with the impact of a tidal wave, washing over and through her. She screamed as shards of electrical pulses ripped through her body jerking her in all directions. Clancy's name slipped out on another wave of sensation, before someone groaned.

Clancy? Ty?

Who the hell cared? Not her. Instead she was consumed by the strength and force of the earth-shattering climax. The slapping of skin against skin, pounding impacts from the front and back, made her heart feel like it would jump from her chest. A muffled sob escaped her trembling lips.

As if it were choreographed, Clancy released a throaty growl and went rigid. Ty followed in his footsteps. Both their cocks jerked several times, the feeling unbelievable, and then they stilled.

After a moment Ty collapsed on top of her. For several heartbeats they lay like a big pile of puppies, before he moaned softly and rolled off her, but not before kissing her cheek.

Sprawling on his back, he threw an arm over his eyes as if to shade them. "Damn, baby. You're unbelievable."

Clancy remained quiet. Instead he tightened his hold around her. And God help her. It felt right, so right.

Sparks of desire continued to dance across Clancy's skin. His pulse had yet to ease its erratic pace, while his arms wouldn't release Tess even if he wanted. At the moment he had climaxed, he had been unconscious of the external world. Nothing and no one existed but the two of them. In a matter of seconds, what had been the most exhilarating moment had became the most consuming peace. One he had never felt before.

Hell. He had even lost sight of Ty fucking her from behind.

The thought of his friend lying beside them made Clancy tense. Then Tess squirmed, reminding him that his flaccid dick was still inside her. Nestled atop him, she rested her head against his chest as if they had been in this intimate position a million times before.

Smoothing his palm over her ass, before tracing a path along her spine, he speared his fingers into her silky hair, bringing a fist full of it to his nose. He breathed the fruity fragrance, finding it intoxicating, a scent he would never forget—like this woman.

From out of nowhere a strange wave of emotions swept over him, catching him unaware. He froze, unable to move.

Clancy didn't want this woman for just a frivolous affair. He wanted her here, in his bed, his home and his life. He had never thought of a woman in that vein. The recognition rattled and confused him. Sex had always been about sex, never about forever. It should have been no different with Tess, but dammit it was.

Shaken, Clancy released his hold on her. He didn't want Tess or Ty realizing his discomfort, but he had to get away, needed some time to think about what was going on with him.

Clancy eased out from beneath her. Her eyes were still closed as she snuggled against his pillow like a kitten, hugging it before she released a soft purr of contentment. When she inhaled, smiled and buried deeper within his pillow, he knew she found his scent pleasant and for some reason that thrilled and scared him.

Moving to the edge of the bed, he continued to watch her. Her breasts were full, nipples tight and erect, and her lips were kiss-swollen. Clancy leaned forward and licked the tender area of her throat where her pulse beat, loving the salty taste, before he realized what he'd done. A half-assed chuckle filled with reproach slipped quietly from his mouth. But not silent enough that Ty didn't adjust his arm and peer out at him with one eye.

Fuck. Quickly getting to his feet, Clancy padded across the room to the bathroom, not bothering to shut the door behind him.

Resting his hands on the edge of the sink, he stared into the mirror. *What the hell is happening to me?* He was a man destined to be alone and here he was playing with fire.

Without a second thought, he turned on the faucet and began to splash cold water on his face, but it didn't make him feel better. Whatever fancy he had with Tess had to be squelched and fast.

After removing the condom, he flushed it down the commode and then cleaned up. Anxiety crawled like bugs across his skin. He rolled his shoulders, attempting to relax, failing, but what the hell. In a last-ditch effort, he ran his fingers through his hair, took a deep breath and exited, but not before mentally putting on a coat of swaggering courage.

"Thirsty?" *Yeah!* To his ears he sounded pretty normal, if not just a little cocky, and why shouldn't he be? Tess had completely lost control in his arms. *Yeah.* He was feeling a little better.

Ty sat up, pushing to his feet. "I could use a beer." He headed to the bathroom.

Clancy glanced at Tess.

Frowning, she gazed up at the ceiling. "What are those for?" She was looking at a set of D-rings used for various activities, which included ropes and chains.

"Those are for another time." Ty's muffled voice came from the bathroom.

"Uh. Boys, there won't be another time." Tess pulled the dark burgundy comforter up, hiding behind it like it was a shield.

"What?" Ty stuck his head from around the door. He disappeared for only a second, before he strutted into the room.

"I...well..."

"What she's trying to say is she's afraid our tainted reputation will sully hers." Okay. So maybe Clancy was speaking about himself, his family's dark history. Still, speaking the truth hurt more than it should have. It wasn't the first time he'd got tangled up with a woman too good for him.

Clancy knew he was right when she had the good sense to blush. Anger and shame collided like freight trains smashing head on inside him. Heat traveled from his neck to his ears, stinging them, the burn driving his hand up to rub the back of his neck.

This fuckin' sucks. His chest tightened. No matter how difficult it was for him to admit, Tess would be better off if they made a quick, clean break.

"It's not that," she insisted, but the pink in her cheeks deepened. "It's my brother, sisters, my job. I can't be—"

"—associated with our kind." Clancy finished her statement with a little more bite in his tone than he had expected.

Tess flinched.

Silently cursing himself, he turned his back to her momentarily and walked into the closet, needing once again to have space between them. Clancy hadn't meant to snap at her. He was mad at himself for letting things get so out of control.

Dammit. Why hadn't he kept his hands in his pockets?

When he yanked a pair of jeans off a hanger, the support flew across the walk-in area, striking the wall. *Shit.* Now it would sound as if he were throwing things around, having a temper tantrum. Dejected, he crammed one leg into the pants, and then the other, pulling them up his hips. He didn't bother fastening them as he returned to face the music.

Tess hadn't moved from the bed. She still gripped the comforter to her chest, her disquiet unnerving, until she spoke.

"About Saturday—"

"I said I'd help you."

Her mouth snapped shut, her eyes widening in surprise.

Clancy briefly closed his eyes, wishing he'd just kept his mouth shut. No matter how he felt, she was his neighbor—neighbors helped each other and she needed his assistance.

Ty glanced toward Clancy. "Saturday?"

"Tess and her brother are new to ranching, as well as raising and breeding cattle. I suggested that they take a look at your setup this weekend. Meant to mention it tonight, but things—" He shrugged. "Your family built your ranch from the ground up, while I inherited mine." Why did that sound like an apology?

The Petersons' ranch worked to support itself, while he had unlimited funds to run his. He could take a drought or disease and work through them, while Ty's family had to accommodate for Murphy's Law's occasional visits.

"I have some ideas I'll share with them when they come to my place."

"Sure." Ty slid his gaze to Tess. "That is, as long as that brother of yours keeps his hands to himself." He winked at her, lightening the moment. "What time would be good for you?"

Before Tess answered, Clancy darted for the door. "I'll get us those beers." When he entered the hall, he took a calming breath. Blowing it out, he headed for the kitchen.

Wedging the refrigeration open, he grabbed three beers. He was popping the top on one when Ty entered the room, dressed in jeans.

"Make that two. She's gone."

Clancy silently nodded, handing Ty a frosty bottle.

The man took a long pull of the beer, and then leaned against the sink counter. "So..."

Pressure released, a slow hiss, as Clancy twisted the top off his drink. He tipped the bottle to his lips, spilling the rich amber into his mouth and down his parched throat, before he responded.

"What?"

"Man. That was so not like you. What's going on?"

Stabbing his fingers through his hair, he remained quiet. What the hell was he supposed to say, that within a week he had fallen for a woman who could never be his? That he wished he came from different stock? That if he could he'd wrap his arms around Tess and never let her go? *Nah.*

"You know." Clancy casually propped a shoulder against the cool refrigerator and took another drink. "Bad week."

From the skeptical gleam in Ty's eyes, Clancy figured he wasn't fooling anyone but himself.

Chapter Ten

Gray clouds crowded the moon. A slight drizzle fell upon Tess, the clean scent of rain rushing over her as she climbed into her car seeking shelter and warmth and maybe even escape. Slamming the door shut, she closed her eyes and sat quietly behind the steering wheel. Tears of regret swelled, threatening to break through the impenetrable wall of determination she had erected when she walked out of Clancy's house. It didn't matter what or who she wanted. She had to think of Rose, Rachel and Levi first and foremost.

Her eyelids rose on a curse. "Shit!" Her palm struck the wheel, hard, sending a sting through her hand. She hadn't resolved the one thing she had set out to do tonight—find out what happened to Levi. The only thing she had accomplished was pissing off the one person who could help her.

She shook her head discouragingly.

How could she blame Clancy for his incriminating glare or his harsh tone? She had insulted him and his friend. To make it worse, she had taken what they had to offer and then threw their infamous reputation back in their face. A caustic laugh burst from her mouth. She was no better than them, because she enjoyed every single second. In fact, her body still hummed from their touch, their kisses. They had loved her so completely, so thoroughly, she couldn't have asked for anything more, except perhaps another go at it. One thing she knew for sure, tonight would be one night she would never forget.

Switching the key on, she started the engine, not hesitating to cram it into gear. But as she pulled out of the drive, she looked back in the rearview mirror. Clancy stood on the porch cast in bright light as if he were an avenging angel, one who saw her for what she really was—a fraud.

Before her parents had been killed, she had it all—parties, travel, friends and plenty of men in her life. Not to mention sex, until that fateful night when her existence changed forever. Now there were three other people who counted on her, needed and depended upon her. A tear rolled down her cheek and she swiped it away, sucking in an unsteady breath.

Glancing at the clock radio on the dashboard as she maneuvered the car down her drive, she noted it was two o'clock in the morning. Why hadn't she just stayed home?

The lights were still on in the living room when she climbed out of the car. Through the closed curtains she saw a shadow moving about. Quickly, she headed for the door, finding it unlocked. Pushing it open, she stepped inside to find Levi sitting on the coach, his head bowed, resting in his palms. When he heard her, he glanced her way.

"I really screwed up," he moaned.

Tess hung her keys on the board and walked to the sofa, taking a seat beside him. "Why?"

"I don't know." He shunned direct eye contact with her. "Guess, I needed to unwind."

"Levi, don't lie to me. This isn't the first time."

"Fuck."

She raised a brow. No. Unlike an ostrich with its head in the sand hiding from the truth, Tess knew her brother cursed, but he had never done so in front of her.

"What's going on?" The need to take him into her arms, console him, rose, but she kept her distance. Levi had to realize how his actions affected the entire family. She also didn't want to give the impression she condoned what he'd done.

"Tess, you need me here—not at college." Even through red eyes she could see how desperately he wanted to remain home and work the ranch. A ranch that may not be as productive as they had first envisioned.

"We've talked about this. You need an education for this to work. If something goes wrong with the ranch, we need backup. Your education will provide that."

Tess couldn't help wondering what had happened to push him to the breaking point. The thought had just slipped through her mind when he dug into his pocket and pulled out a crumpled envelope. Silently, he handed it to her.

When she saw Rice University on the outside of the envelope, her gaze rose to meet Levi's. Goose bumps raced across her skin. "Really?"

Levi nodded.

This time she let her emotions have rein. Tears of pride swelled and fell. "Dad—" She choked, then with trembling hands retrieved the enclosed letter of acceptance. "It was his dream that you attend the same college he did."

"I know." But there was no enthusiasm in her brother's voice.

That's when Tess realized how much pressure Levi must be under. The pain in his eyes confirmed it, before he looked away.

"It—" The word caught in his throat.

"It was Dad's dream—not yours."

He nodded.

Tess placed her hand on his shoulder and felt the tremor that assailed him. He was crying—her brother who had been so strong during the death of their parents, was bawling like a baby.

She sucked in a shuddering breath as a sob slipped out. "Oh God, Levi. I'm so sorry." He had to be torn between wanting one thing, while also wanting to fulfill their father's dream. Not unlike the responsibility that weighed so heavily on her. Her parents had expected her to step in if something ever happened to them, to protect Rose, Rachel and Levi, and to ensure that each of them received a good education.

Wrapping her arms around him, she pressed her cheek against his back. Together they wept for their parents, their lonely lives, and the losses that just seemed to keep coming.

When their tears began to lighten, she squeezed him. "We'll work this out, but you have to make me a promise."

He turned in her arms. "What?"

"No more drinking. Levi—" She bit her bottom lip, fighting for control. When she spoke again, her voice dipped into a whisper. "I can't lose you."

He stood up, taking her with him, before pulling her into his embrace. "You won't lose me, Tess. I promise."

Tess looked up through a veil of tears. "Still, I want to hear you say you won't drink."

"I won't."

She frowned, stepping out of his arms. "Levi?"

"Dammit, Tess." He rubbed his chin. "Everyone does it."

"Noooo." She strung out the word. "Every underage person doesn't drink." She folded her arms across her chest as she pinned him with a glare.

He released an exasperated breath. "All right. I won't drink."

"That includes drugs."

His eyes widened in disbelief. "*Tess!*"

"I know. I'm just covering all the possibilities, closing any loopholes you might be intrigued to investigate."

Again, he shook his head. "I can't believe you even thought I'd do something like that."

"I never thought I'd have our next-door neighbor hauling your drunken ass home. Which reminds me, what was this fighting all about?"

"It was just a misunderstanding."

She knew her skeptical expression hit its mark when Levi blushed and a sheepish grin crept across his face.

"Uhhh. I was sort of hitting on some guy's woman."

"And Ty Peterson?"

"Well, I might have told him that his sister was hot."

"Oh, Levi." Broken laughter followed. She dropped her arms to her sides. Girls. She really didn't want to deal with this.

"Well, she is. Prettiest little gal in San Antonio."

"Fine, but if you want to keep your head on your shoulders you might think of staying away from her. We have an appointment to tour the Peterson's ranch on Saturday and I expect you be a perfect gentleman."

"Saturday? How did you manage that?" He paused, a scowl wrinkling his forehead as he glanced at the wall clock. "It's almost two forty-five. Where have you been, Tess?"

This time it was her turn to blush. Heat skipped across her cheeks. "Trying to find out what happened to you."

"That doesn't answer my question."

Defensively, she pressed her palms to her hips. "I was paving the way for visits to the Petersons and Wisemans." Okay, maybe that wasn't exactly what she was doing. "What do you think I was doing? I went to Clancy's to apologize and find out more of what happened tonight, but it seems he had no idea."

Levi gave her a suspicious once-over. "The conversation could have waited until the morning."

"Technically it is morning."

"You know what I mean."

"Yeah. I do. And if we don't get some sleep, neither of us will be any good to anyone tomorrow. So get!"

He hesitated and she could see questions building in his foggy head. "How long were you at Wiseman's?"

"Levi, get your butt up those stairs."

As she watched him walk away swaying, she couldn't help wondering what would have happened if Clancy hadn't been there to rescue her brother.

Leaning lazily against the kitchen doorjamb, Ty took a long pull off his beer. "Tess Gilmore is a prize filly." He leveled a hard stare on Clancy. "You're not gonna let this one slip through your fingers, are you?"

Clancy presented his friend with his back. Grabbing a dishcloth, he wiped down the counter, before hooking three bottles between the fingers of one hand. "You heard her. Tonight was a first and last." He wrenched the pantry door open, tossing the empties into the trashcan. The glass clinked together as one of them shattered.

"You know as well as I do, she enjoyed tonight. All she needs is a little coaxing."

"The woman's made up her mind." Clancy slammed the door a little too hard. "She went slumming tonight, buddy. You. Her. Me. Not going to happen again."

Ty pushed away from the wall walking toward the pantry. He opened the door and disposed of his bottle. "So how about that ride back to my truck?"

"It's late. Why don't you crash here?"

"Love to, but you're not my type."

Clancy picked up the closest thing to him other than his beer, which was the scouring pad, and chucked it at the teasing man.

Ty flinched. Chuckling, he caught the sponge, wasting no time to hurl it back.

For the first time since Tess left, Clancy's heart lightened. "Guest room, gay-boy," he growled.

Ty's eyes twinkled with mischief. "Uh shucks, darlin'." His whiskey-smooth voice softened. "Don't be like that." Then he blew Clancy a kiss.

Clancy rolled his tired eyes. No wonder Wade felt like horsewhipping his brother half the time. Ty had a way of taking everything and making a jest. Yet his carefree nature was one of the things Clancy enjoyed the most about the man.

"Think I'll hit the hay." Retrieving his drink from the counter, he swallowed the remainder and sat it back down. "I'm heading down to Austin to tomorrow to look at a couple of horses."

Ty followed him out of the kitchen. "Think I'll join you."

Quietly they walked through the living room and down the hall. When they came to the first guest room, Ty disappeared within without a word. Clancy continued to his own bedroom, closing the door behind him.

He glanced at the cold, gray embers in the hearth and walked over to the fireplace, squatting before it before reaching for the tinder. In seconds he had kindled the flames, then he placed another log atop. His mind blank, he stared into the crackling blaze, warmth spreading across his face as the fresh scent of pine filled the room. An image of him and Tess lying before the flickering fire materialized. He popped to his feet and the figment dissolved. Last thing he needed was the picture of her sweet body, her memory in his head as he fell asleep.

After disrobing, he laid his jeans over a chair and plopped down upon the bed, his head striking the soft down of his pillow. Immediately he was assailed by Tess's feminine scent. She was all over his sheets, his pillow, and when he threw an arm over his eyes, she was there on his skin. Drawing his arm off his face, he tossed and turned, trying to find comfort to no avail. Unless he showered and changed rooms, he would spend tonight drenched in her memory.

He yawned, his ears popping. When they cleared he could have sworn he heard *Uh. Boys, there won't be another time.* Tess's long, blonde hair mussed as she hid behind his dark burgundy comforter made him want to reach out and strip her of her shield. Do exactly what Ty had suggested. Coax the woman back into his arms. Instead he rolled over and pinched his eyelids tightly together.

A sensation, so light and brief, tickled Clancy's nose. Caught between the space of slumber and semi-consciousness, he scrunched his face and heard tinkling laughter.

"Are you an angel?"

Tess's sexy voice bled through Clancy's foggy mind, pulling him awake, but not before another peel of laughter greeted him. When his heavy eyelids rose, her beautiful face hovered over him. Full, voluptuous lips eased into a sexy smile.

"Did you fall from Heaven?" she breathed, sending his heart reeling.

He chuckled, remembering the words he'd spoken to her when they first met. "Darlin', that's my line." Reaching for her, he circled her slender waist and she went willingly into his arms. "I need you naked."

"Anything you want." The jeans and sweater she had been wearing dissolved, her naked body sliding over his.

"Tell me this is real." His throat thickened with emotion. "Tell me you'll never leave me."

She pressed her lips to his, her touch so tender he thought perhaps it was only his imagination. But then she pulled away. No matter how he grasped to hold on to her, she slipped from his fingers as if she were a ghost, nonexistent.

"Tess? Please."

Sadness filled her eyes. Large blue pools spilled down her cheeks. "You know I can't stay."

"Yes you can." She only had to want to. "Please don't go. Everyone leaves me," he blurted before he could stop himself. His mother had left him. Even though he had hated his father, he too had deserted him. And then there was Jessie.

Feeling raw and dejected, he attempted to rise, but his limbs wouldn't move. No matter how he struggled, he lay helplessly, watching Tess drift farther and farther away.

Clancy woke with a start, shooting straight up in bed, his heart pounding. "Tess!" Her name died upon his tongue. A light sheen of perspiration covered his body, his pulse raced. For a moment he expected to see her lingering in his doorway, but like always he was alone. Always alone. Feeling lost in a sea of emotion, he got to his feet and began to pace.

Damn this vulnerability.

Since he was thirteen, he had never needed anyone. He had everything he'd ever wanted. His life was a testament to that. His ranch was successful. He had friends. He had women when he wanted them. He didn't need anything or anyone and that included Tess.

Hell. The woman came with baggage—two teenage sisters, a brother sewing his oats, and a ranch that may or may not make it.

He ran his fingers through his hair. Even if their paths entwined there was his history.

Clancy gazed at the alarm clock, six beaming back at him. Only three hours of sleep. What would Ty say if he woke him up? Told him to get ready?

"Screw it."

Needing to move around, he dressed, exiting the room with his boots in hand. Once inside the living room, he sat on the couch, sticking a foot into a boot. With a tug he slipped it on. After the final shoe was on, he rose, heading for the door.

As he walked outside, another rainy day met him. The fresh, clean scent surrounded him. He cast a wary glance at the dreary sky and released a half-assed chuckle.

"What? Did you expect anything different?"

He stuck his hands into his jeans pockets and went to look for Milo.

Chapter Eleven

When Saturday rolled around, the big Texas sky opened up with a torrential storm. Ominous black clouds hovered overhead. Bolts of lightning zigzagged across the horizon, as thunder boomed, shaking the heavens. Through a sheet of rain that threatened to never stop, Tess peered out the window. A chill radiated off the glass. She hugged herself. The dreariness outside represented how she felt.

Yesterday had been a mixture of good and bad memories. Her body ached in places that brought a smile to her face, while other flashbacks reduced her tender thoughts to ashes. Still tired from her lack of sleep, a yawn forced her mouth wide. Work had been hell. During quiet times when the children were busy, her eyes had drifted closed, only to be greeted by the picture of two wild cowboys worshiping her body. Her daydreams lasted only a moment before Clancy's crestfallen expression turning to anger imposed upon them.

Her delicate attempts to end their tryst had failed. She had insulted both Clancy and Ty, and no matter how many times she told herself there hadn't been any alternative, she still felt like shit.

The abrupt ringing of the telephone jarred her concentration, but it didn't sway her from where she stood. Neither did the second ring or the third. On the fourth ring, someone picked up the irritating thing.

"Yeah. Sure." Levi's voice cut through her melancholy. "No problem. I completely understand. Tess?"

She glanced over a shoulder.

Levi held a palm over the receiver. "It's Wiseman. Change of plans. He wants to know if next weekend is okay?"

Tess nodded.

Clancy's call had been anticipated. In all honesty, she was thankful for the reprieve. In fact, if it weren't that her family needed the rancher's guidance, she would have declined the invitation entirely.

The telephone clinked as Levi returned it to its cradle. "This sucks. When is this rain supposed to stop?"

"Weatherman says we're in for a series of storms off and on throughout the week," she responded.

A scream came from upstairs, followed by a host of arguing. The girls were at it again. Cabin fever. The rain was getting to them all.

Releasing the curtain to let it fall before the window, Tess pivoted. "That's it. Tell the girls to get ready. We're going to the mall and out for lunch."

"But—"

"Just do it, Levi. If we don't get out of the house, we'll all go stir crazy."

Tess watched Levi disappear down the hall, before she went to secure the backdoor. When she heard a squeal of delight, she knew she'd made a good call. Maybe they would even take in a movie. As she drifted back into the living room, she heard hurried footsteps clambering down the hollow stairs and she raised her sight.

Rose hopped to the bottom of the steps. "Let's go to Macy's. Their cosmetics are on sale."

"No. Dillard's," Rachel countered. "I need a new pair of shoes."

Tess clenched her jaws together. Of course they would be at odds. "We can go both places." She grabbed her purse and jacket off the end table.

"I'll drive," Levi offered.

Digging in her bag, she located her keys and gave them a toss. Levi caught them midair with one hand. Pride rose in her as he moved to the door, holding it open for them. Their parents would be so proud of the man he had become. She was still preening when Rose shot out into the rain. She jerked on the car door only to find it still locked.

Her head snapped up. "Levi!"

He chuckled. "Sorry." Pressing the button on the remote control, he unlocked the doors with a click and Rose scrambled inside.

Next Rachel darted into the rain, Tess hot on her heels, her jacket in the bend of her arm. Levi was the last to enter, sliding behind the wheel looking like a drowned rat. Glancing in the mirror, Tess discovered the miserable weather had left its mark on all of them. She didn't look any better than her siblings.

Rose slapped the back of Levi's head, nearly knocking off his hat. "I'm soaked."

"Hey. It was an oversight." Sheepishly, he glanced Tess's way. "What?"

She flashed him her best *sure-it-was* expression.

His eyes twinkled with mischief. He pinched his lips together, fighting the grin behind them, before he turned the key and the engine roared to life. As he shifted the car into gear, a low rumble caught her attention, as well as her brother's and sisters'. No one spoke or moved as the resonating sound grew louder and louder. It wasn't thunder or Mother Nature wielding her mighty hand. Still, Tess knew it didn't sound good. Her premonition was confirmed when the earth's growl burst free along with a jet stream of water that blew eight feet into the air ten feet away from the house.

The girls released a tight scream from the backseat of the car. Levi cursed, his fingers curling tighter around the steering wheel. Tess hadn't realized she held her breath until she gasped.

"It's the main line." He reached for his door, opened it and climbed out.

Without pausing, Tess followed Levi out of the vehicle, mud squishing beneath her shoes. A wave of helplessness rippled over her as she stopped beside him. "What are we going to do?"

"I don't know." His deflated expression matched how she felt.

The car door slammed twice. Rose and Rachel squealed as they made their way back into the house.

So much for their outing.

It seemed like forever that she and Levi stood like idiots in the pouring rain. Their eyes were pinned on the geyser, as if staring at it would make it disappear or a stroke of genius would strike them before lightning.

"Perhaps you should turn the water off."

Tess and Levi jumped, spinning around to see Clancy standing behind them. Unlike them, he had dressed for the climate. An expensive black oilskin coat hung just above his ankles and galoshes. Even a rain cover protected his Stetson.

"I was driving by. Thought I could be of assistance. Do you know where your shutoff valve is?"

Levi's shoulders fell. "Yeah." He shook his head with an expression that screamed dumbass. Then he took a step, sliding and almost losing his footing. After flailing about, he righted himself and took a careful step forward, followed by another, until he disappeared around the side of the house.

Clancy started to shrug out of his coat. "Here."

"Please. No. I'm already soaked to the bone. You're not."

He stared at her quietly, before adding, "Are you sure?"

"Yes—"

A sudden crack of thunder made Tess's pulse leap, as well as her body. Her feet slipped. For a heartbeat she thought she'd fall. Instead, she found herself in Clancy's arms, clinging to him. His breath brushed over her face. Their mouths so close all she had to do was pucker her lips. When she realized where her thoughts were taking her, heat singed her cheeks.

"Oh God. I'm sorry."

She nervously eased back, putting distance between them, but the damage was already done. His clean, soapy scent filled her lungs. Memories of being in his arms, his touch and kiss, rushed through her mind. Cue the wind that blew the rain sideways and a chill slithered up her spine. Tess fought the urge to climb back into his warm embrace, when what she really needed at the moment was to keep her wits about her and focus on the problem—a broken water line.

Readjusting his coat, he directed his attention to the fountain of water before them. Slowly it began to recede, dropping in height, until it bubbled beneath the turbid pond that had accumulated around the break.

When she pushed the air from her lungs, she groaned. "I can't believe this."

He glanced over a shoulder, a tight expression on his handsome face.

Crap. Had he misinterpreted her words?

"The leak," she clarified. "Do plumbers work on weekends?"

"No need. Levi and I can take care of it."

Tess raised her gaze, catching him staring at her chest. He quickly straightened his head, again glancing down at the pooling water.

Dammit. Her thin white sweater lay almost transparent, molding her body like a second skin, to reveal the lacy bra with small pink roses beneath.

She crossed her arms over her breasts. "We can't ask that of you."

"You want to go the entire weekend without water?"

No. That wouldn't do either.

Before she could think of an alternative, Levi came splashing up to them. Her poor brother's hat lay limp on his head. The brim tilted so that the rain sluiced down the edge right down the back of his shirt.

"What now?" He shivered.

Clancy turned. "We'll need a couple of shovels, a bucket and a large umbrella or a tarp we can work under. Some clean dry towels you won't mind throwing away." He paused. "That should do. In the meantime, I'll get my stuff." Without another word he pivoted and made tracks to his truck.

"Let's go." She started toward the barn.

Catching up with her, Levi grabbed her arm, pulling her to a stop. "I can do this. Go into the house."

The rain had lessened, but they couldn't count on it to behave. The more help they had the better. Besides, like it or not, she had to learn every in and out of this ranch, water lines being one of them.

"We're in this together—good or bad."

He forced a smile. "Rain or shine?"

"Yeah, yeah. C'mon."

By the time they had retrieved all the items Clancy had requested and staked a tarp to work under, his big black truck rolled into their driveway. He got out and retrieved a toolbox, something that looked like a rolled-up exercise mat, and a couple of different sizes of bright copper piping from the bed of his vehicle.

As he approached, a frown tugged at the corners of his mouth. "Tess, you need to get inside, before you get chilled."

She wanted to say, "Too late," but didn't. Instead she hid the shiver that slithered through her. "I'm fine. What do we have to do next?"

"You *have* to get your butt in the house and at least get something dry on. Both of you." His firm tone left no room for argument.

Without responding, she and Levi hightailed it to the house.

Stomping muddy feet at the front door, they slipped off their boots before entering. Water rolled off their clothes, pooling on the floor.

"Is that Clancy outside? Is he helping?"

Bless Rose. Their sister had a pile of towels waiting beside the door.

Tess nodded as she grabbed a towel, blotting her face and attempting to lessen the mess she was making on the floor.

"Go on up and change. Rachel and I will clean up." Without further encouragement from Rose, Tess and Levi headed up the stairs.

Inside her bedroom, she tugged off her sweater, carrying it into the bathroom. Her wet jeans didn't come off so easily. After pushing and wiggling, she finally managed to shed herself of the damn pants. Flinging the sodden garments across the bathtub, she moved to her closet and selected a new outfit along with a slicker and galoshes.

In no time, she was back in the rain and wind, staring at a man who she would rather be curled up on a coach next to, sipping hot rum punch, than standing ankle-deep in muck.

Building a berm around the work area to keep the rain out, Clancy glanced up to find Tess staring at him. The second their eyes met, she looked away and reached for the other shovel. A black galosh against the footrest, she buried the blade into the soft ground. Her eyes widened as she raised the heavy mud, but she didn't complain, only packed the sludge along the path he'd started and continued to help.

One more thing about her that he found intriguing. Although she had been raised in the city, she wasn't afraid to get her hands dirty. Dedicated. She wanted to learn about ranching, and evidently fixing water lines. Maybe *wanted* wasn't the right term, she *needed* to learn, and nothing or no one would stand between her and the success of this place.

Tess's determination cut like a two-sided blade. On one hand, Clancy admired her grit. On the other, it was the crux of their problems. He paused, shovel midair. Who the hell was he kidding? This was his doing, his *reputation*, that stood between them.

"Tess. Let me do that."

Levi's presence shattered Clancy's self-abasement. Instead of the sodden cowboy hat, the boy wore a slicker with a hood. Like his sister, he had chosen more appropriate footwear.

"I can do it—"

Levi grabbed the shovel handle, but Tess wouldn't release it. He tugged. "For once, sis, don't argue with me."

"Fine." She let go. "What can I do?"

When Levi remained quiet, Clancy emptied his blade and drew his attention to her. "We'll need to dig to find the break. You can bail the water." He jammed the shovel into the ground and fetched the rolled kneepad, before handing it to her. "Use this. It'll keep you from getting muddy."

It took another five minutes to finish the berm, and then he and Levi began to uncover the break, digging far enough beneath the pipe to allow them space to maneuver. With each shovel-full of mud extracted, Tess bailed the water. In no time, Clancy replaced Tess on the matt.

Cleaning the mud off the pipe with a towel, he began to explain the process. "Your main water line is a two-inch copper pipe coming off your well. It reduces down to three-quarters at your house. Cut past the break a couple of inches on each side." He used a pair of tube cutters and sliced the corroded pipe. Water oozed from each end. "The extension will be slightly shorter to accommodate your sleeves."

Damn. This was difficult. He'd never had to explain the steps as he worked. Yet both Levi and Tess were diligent students, watching and listening carefully.

After Clancy cut a length of copper from the pipe he brought with him, he set it aside before using an emery cloth to smooth the old pipe until it shone like new. Reaching for a small can, he twisted the lid open and extracted the brush on the end. "Use flux to grease the outside of each section of pipe and the inside of each sleeve. Then slip the sleeves onto each end of pipe and connect them." It took a little time to wiggle the pieces on, but when he succeeded, he reached for his torch, lighting it with the lighter in his toolbox. A blue flame burst from the end. "Now we'll solder the sleeves." When he was finished, he got to his feet and addressed Levi. "Turn the water back on so we can check for leaks."

As the young man slipped away, Rose and Rachel approached, grins on their pretty faces. That's when he noticed the rain had stopped. The sun shyly peeked from between the dark clouds.

"Hey, Clancy," they each said.

"Hi, girls."

They fidgeted. Rose elbowed Rachel in the side and the girl returned the jab.

Tess frowned. "What are you two up to?"

"Rose?" Rachel's eyes widened.

Even Clancy could detect the note of false innocence in her voice, but he loved watching the interplay of this family unit. Nothing appeared to get past Tess—well, maybe the small issue with Levi the other night. Still, she amazed him. She was intelligent and intuitive, if not just a little suspicious.

"Rose? Rachel?" she growled.

"Really. We just prepared lunch for Clancy. For helping us," Rose quickly added. "Say you'll stay."

"Please," Rachel begged.

"That was very thoughtful." Tess turned on the ball of her galoshes and raised her wary sight to meet his. "You will join us?"

Lost in her gaze, he said yes before he realized it. Still fixated on her mesmerizing eyes, he didn't hear Levi's return until he spoke.

"Any leaks?"

Clancy blinked, dropping his gaze to the ground to find the pipe still dry. "Looks like we did it."

Levi released a relieved breath before he glanced at Tess. "What's wrong?"

"Wrong?" Now it was her turn to blink. "Uh. Nothing." Her brows furrowed. "Let's clean up." She bent over and picked up a shovel. "The girls have prepared lunch."

"Good. I'm hungry," her brother grumbled. "You're staying aren't you, Clancy?"

"Yes. He's staying," Tess answered before he could. "Girls." She motioned to her sisters to retrieve the towels. "We need to thank him properly for his assistance."

A pang tightened Clancy's chest. He didn't want to join them out of obligation. He longed to be a part of their family.

The abrupt thought drew him up short. It struck him hard enough that he stumbled when he attempted to lift his toolbox. Several items fell out, splashing into a puddle. Pausing, he fought to regain his composure. He'd never considered being a part of anyone's family. The closest he'd ever come was with Wade and Ty's family, and of course Jessie. Still he had always felt isolated, like he didn't belong. But here, with Tess, something was different.

Unease skittered over his skin. He started to skim through the water for his tools. "I should be going—"

"But you said you'd stay," Rachel insisted.

"Yeah," Rose chimed.

Tess cocked a questioning brow.

Dammit. He felt the need to retreat, but the disappointment on Rose's and Rachel's faces stopped him. His fingers closed around a wrench and he lifted it from the water, drying it before he placed it back into the chest.

Levi sidled up beside him, leaning down to get the kneepad. As he rolled and fastened it, he flashed Clancy a weak smile. "When they make up their mind, there's no getting around them. Believe me, you're staying for lunch." Then he grabbed the toolbox and remaining copper piping from Clancy and trotted off to the truck.

Clancy felt at odds with the situation, so he changed the subject. "You should probably leave the pipe uncovered until tomorrow. Just to ensure another leak doesn't spring free."

"That makes sense." Tess scanned the area. "We'll leave the tarp as well. Rachel, show Clancy where he can clean up. Levi and I will finish up here."

He didn't get the opportunity to argue as both girls, arms full of unused towels, corralled him on each side and very successfully guided him away.

Clancy had forgotten what fifteen-year-old girls were like. If they weren't chattering, they were giggling. Each of them attempted to outdo the other for his attention, which he found flattering. Now, if only Tess felt the same way about him, he could die a happy man.

Standing before the front door, Rose pulled to a halt and started toeing off her galoshes, followed by Rachel. He did the same, stepping into the house in his stocking feet. Immediately he felt the warmth, the love in their house that his home lacked. And maybe that was his fault, because the pictures of him and his parents had long since been buried in the attic. He wanted no remembrance of his childhood and the people who hadn't cared enough to stick around.

"Bathroom?" he asked.

"Second door on the left," Rose answered.

"Thanks." He didn't wait for a response. As a wave of remorse threatened to swamp him, he shook it off and closed the door behind him.

After taking off his hat, he splashed cold water in his face and washed his hands, toweling them dry. Clancy felt like a new man. That is until he opened the door and ran smack dab into Tess, his arms circling her to steadying her. For a moment they simply stared at each other.

"I should go," he whispered.

She didn't make any attempt to pull away. Her palms were warm against his chest. "No. Stay."

"Are you sure?" Clancy wanted to kiss her so badly he could almost taste her sweet, sweet lips against his. He inched closer, softly skimming his nose along hers.

She briefly closed her eyes. For a split-second he thought she would close the distance between their mouths, but she didn't. Instead, she breathed, "No. I'm not sure, but the girls would be crushed if you left."

"What about you, Tess? Would you be crushed?"

Chapter Twelve

Yes. God. Yes.

Tess barely held back the cry that echoed through her. She wanted Clancy to stay for lunch, then again, she didn't. Her emotions were all over the place. It was like playing with fire. Someone was going to get burned and that someone would be her.

"*Tess!* Can we use the china?" Rose hollered from another room.

"Yes," she hissed. Yet her attention wasn't on what her sister asked, but the man so close that all she had to do was pucker and their mouths would touch. Sliding her tongue between her parched lips, she wet them. The movement drew Clancy's hungry gaze, sending her pulse in overdrive. Heat simmered in his eyes. He wanted to kiss her. She knew this because she felt the same.

The man could kiss. Hell, he could make her body sing like it had never sung before.

Instead of reaching for what she wanted, she eased out of his arms. "I better clean up."

"I think we should talk about this thing between us."

This thing? What was this thing? Lust? A fleeting attraction? Something that would end as quickly as it started?

She shook her head. "You and I both know this thing we feel is fleeting and would never work. Besides, I don't have time for a man. My focus is on my brother and sisters. Let's not make it worse."

Irony filled his quiet chuckle. "Worse?" He stood silently staring at her as if his mind were running a mile a minute. Then, without another word, he squared his hat upon his head and pivoted, walking away.

Regret swam through her, but she had no choice. Instead, she took one last, longing look, and entered the bathroom. Staring into the mirror, she asked herself, "What is wrong with me?" Never had there been a man who called to her like Clancy. Maybe she was lonely. Maybe she wanted what she couldn't have. And maybe she just needed someone to hold her. Her hands were shaking when she placed them beneath the water.

After cleaning up, she exited the bathroom. Her footsteps felt heavy as she entered the living room, moving onward to the dining room. Her mother's crystal and china lay upon the table. Napkin's neatly pleated on each plate just like her mother used to fold them.

A sigh released.

She ran a finger along the delicate edge of one of the plates. At that moment she was eight, sitting on her mother's lap and staring into the china cabinet. Her mother's soft voice danced in her ears, explaining the difficulties her great-great-grandmother endured bringing the china over from Germany. Unexpected tears gathered behind Tess's eyelids, making her nose tingle and her face heat.

"You okay?"

Turning to see Clancy standing in the doorway, she sucked in a trembling breath. "I miss them."

A shadow rippled over his eyes. "Your pain will lessen with time."

Concern tugged at her brows. "You too?"

His expression went blank, but the veins in his neck began to slowly protrude. "My mother left. My father was killed the next day."

She gasped in disbelief. "Killed?"

"A Brahma. He tried to ride the bull drunk." A hint of bitterness seeped out behind his detachment.

Tess didn't know who moved first, but they stood before each other at the foot of the table.

"How old were you?" she asked.

"Fourteen." His jaw seesawed. "An uncle took me in. Raised me."

He had been so young.

"I'm so sorry." She raised her hand, tenderly stroking his cheek, but he turned away from her.

"You learn to live with it."

Live with it? How could she? How could he? But that was exactly what they were doing—living with it.

Her sisters' voices rose as they neared the dining room. When they entered, both glanced at Tess, and then pulled to an abrupt halt.

"Everything all right?" Rose moved forward and set the bowl of salad she held upon the table.

"Fine." Hoping to focus on something other than the heaviness in the room, Tess attempted a smile that faltered when she looked down at the place settings. "The table looks b-beautiful." Her eyes began to water.

"Tess. We're sorry." Rachel sat a large plate of spaghetti down, before she moved toward Tess. "We didn't think." She snaked her arms around her.

Entering the room, Levi took in the scene. "Dammit." Without another word, he went straight to her. Nudging Rachel aside, he took Tess into his arms. His chin rested lightly against atop of her head. "They didn't think, sis."

She inhaled a shuddering breath. "I'm being silly." Her show of weakness made Rachel's chin quiver. Rose teared up. Even Levi's grip tightened around her.

How embarrassing. Pushing out of Levi's arms, she swiped angrily at her moist eyes. "I'm sorry."

"Darlin', you don't have to apologize." Clancy stayed rooted where he stood. "Maybe I should go."

"No. Really." She caught her reflection in the mirror of the china cabinet. Wet eyelashes. Red nose. How wonderful. "Just give me a second." Excusing herself, she headed back to the bathroom.

Sitting on the commode, she allowed herself several minutes to gather her composure. Why did her fortitude waver every time she came in contact with the cowboy? She was still pondering the question when a knock rapped upon the door.

"Sis? You okay?"

"I'm fine, Levi. I'll be there in second."

When she finally heard him step away, she rose and went to the sink. Applying more cosmetics would make it look as if she was trying too hard. No. It was best if she waltzed back into the dining room, head held high, her confidence intact, not caring what Clancy thought.

And that's just what she did.

Taking a seat, she inhaled, but her now stuffy nose didn't allow her to appreciate the rich scent of tomato sauce and spices. "It smells good," she improvised. Yet she wasn't fooling anyone. Four sets of concerned eyes were pinned on her. No one moved or spoke. "What?" She shook out her napkin and sat it in her lap. "I had a nostalgic moment. It's over. Let's eat."

That should have been the end of it, but her siblings weren't buying it. She had been their rock since their parents' death. They weren't used to her falling apart and especially in front of guests.

She attempted to relax the tension in her jaws. "So, Rose and Rachel, did you use Mom's recipe?"

The girls shared cautious glances.

"Y-yes," Rose said warily.

"Clancy, if you like spaghetti you'll enjoy this. Our mother was an excellent cook. The girls are taking after her." With a slight tremor in her grasp, she retrieved her glass of water, steadying her hand. Before taking a sip, she said, "Levi, pass him the salad."

The following silence was unnerving, but she managed to hold it together. She breathed a sigh of relief when silverware clicked against plates and everyone began to eat, but the mood was still somber.

Levi tore off a piece of French bread. "I saw a new Paint in your east pasture." He slathered butter on the slice and took a bite.

Clancy nodded, swallowing before he spoke. "Gypsy is a yearling with champion bloodlines. I picked her up the other day in Austin. When she's old enough I'll breed her with a champion stallion out of Wyoming." He slid his gaze down the table to briefly meet Tess's.

She forced a smile she didn't feel.

Levi took another bite. "She's a beauty."

Lunch continued on with small talk, rising in tone as Rose and Rachel joined in. Pretty soon it was as if nothing had happened, but it had for Tess. She had showed weakness before her siblings and sufficiently closed the door between any sort of personal relationship with Clancy. All in all, it had been a completely horrible day.

As the girls began to clean up, she and Levi walked Clancy out. The rain had stopped. The air smelled clean, fresh. A slight breeze ruffled her hair.

She glanced over to where they had been working on the water line. "I can't thank you enough for what you've done for us."

"Yeah. Thanks." Levi jutted his hand out to Clancy and he accepted it, shaking.

"No need. It was the neighborly thing to do." He slid his gaze toward Tess. "Good-bye."

Her heart fluttered. "Good-bye."

Then he turned and walked away.

While Levi went to inspect the water line, she watched Clancy drive away. Her chest felt heavier and heavier with the distance growing between them.

"Dammit," Clancy cursed, clenching the steering wheel tighter. It seemed like every time he got close to Tess, something inside him knotted up and he forgot who he was. Yet for a brief moment when they stood in her hallway, nose to nose, their lips a breath away, he could have sworn she wanted to kiss him. That she'd felt the same magnetic pull he had. Wanted the same thing he did, but it had only been his foolish pride.

No. Tess Gilmore had her head on straight, her priorities in line, and taking a chance on a worthless cowboy wasn't on her list of things to do. The sooner he realized that, the sooner he could get some much-needed sleep, but it wouldn't be today. He turned his truck toward the Petersons.

Several young colts kicked up their heels as he maneuvered down their driveway. As he approached, he saw Shelby disappear into the barn, Clint Senior behind her. Easing on the brake, Clancy came to a stop and turned the engine off. Within minutes he was out of his vehicle and slipping into the barn.

Silence met him, as well as the sweet scent of hay and oats.

Then he heard a low, guttural moan and Shelby's excited high-pitched wail. "Oh look."

"Shhh..." He didn't need to see the one who responded to know it was Jessie. He'd recognize her voice anywhere.

As he moved down the path of stalls, he saw Shelby peering through the slats of one. Next to her stood Clint Senior and next to him was Madeline, his wife, and finally Jessie. Something inside had caught their attention.

"It's a colt," Wade said from within the stable.

"Darn," Shelby grumbled, while Clint Senior chuckled.

"Whoa, girl," Ty cooed as grunts and shuffling followed.

By the time Clancy stepped next to Shelby, the mare inside had risen and was nosing her baby, a wet little Dunn.

"Clancy!" Shelby yelled, spinning around to hug his waist.

He gazed down at her and his chest squeezed. From the moment her worthless father abandoned her with Jessie, the little urchin had captured his heart.

He placed a finger against his lips, quieting her, and then pointed to the newborn. "Watch."

On wobbly, bent legs, the colt attempted to rise, falling down only to try again. Ty, Wade and Clint Junior stood off to the sides, watching his progress as the womenfolk made soft sounds of encouragement.

"Dry him off." The tall, sixty-three year old man shook his head. Throughout the years, gray had slipped through his brown hair, cut short and neat. "We don't want him to get a chill from this darn weather." Each of his sons grabbed a towel and quickly went to work, as Clint Senior shook Clancy's hand. "Why do these females want to drop their babes in this kind of weather?"

"Hell if I know," he responded, but it was true. There was something about a rainy day that triggered birthing. He'd had two cows drop their calves around five this morning, another mama in the early stages of labor when he had left the house earlier.

Madeline eased up beside him and gave him a tender kiss on the cheek. Then she brushed back a lock of her short, brown hair behind an ear. "What brings you out on a day like this?"

Wade's mother was a local trauma counselor and a sweetheart of a lady. She never ceased to amaze him. There was something warm and inviting about her, from the casual loose sweater and jeans she wore to the gentleness in her voice.

"Just wondering how y'all were getting on in this weather." It was a lie. After leaving the Gilmore's he wanted—no, needed— a sense of family. The Petersons and Jessie were the closest to that he had.

"Hungry?" Madeline asked.

"No thank you, ma'am."

For a second, she quietly scrutinized him with her too astute gaze. Only the slight dip of a brow displayed concern. Before he realized it, he shifted his feet and silently cursed himself for the telltale.

She inhaled, before she took him into her arms and hugged him. "Well, we're so happy you stopped by," she whispered in his ear. "We don't see enough of you. You're like one of my boys. You know that, don't you, Clancy?"

Emotion stung his eyes, threatening to dig its claws into him, but he held on to his dignity by just a thread. "Thank you." The strangled words were almost his undoing. It didn't help that Jessie now had her bright eyes pinned on him.

As Madeline released him, Jessie strolled up beside them. She reached out and grabbed his hand in hers. "Hey, let's take a walk."

Damn. He was pitiful. Were his insecurities tattooed on his fuckin' forehead?

135

When they squeezed through the open barn door, a light mist greeted them. The fresh, clean scent did nothing to ease the chill that slithered through him. Releasing her hand, he pulled the edges of his jacket together and zipped them.

"So... What's up?" she asked, watching him.

"Damn weather puts me on edge."

She chuckled. "Liar." Then she shot him a *you-gonna-stick-to-that-story* expression, but he ignored her, choosing to look away.

Silence engulfed them as they strolled onward.

"You know you're talking, or rather not talking to me, Clancy."

"Yeah. I forgot what a nag you can be."

The punch in the shoulder came from out of nowhere, stinging his arm. He cupped his palm over the spot.

"Owww. What's that for?" he asked.

"You are such a bullheaded man. Something is wrong. We've never kept secrets from each other. Don't tell me you're going to start now."

"It's the weather, Jess. Just makes me a little melancholy."

She cocked her head, her penetrating stare made him uneasy. "No," she simply said, before she added, "You know I love you."

Pulling the brim of his hat down, he choked, "Yeah. I know."

Her fingers closed around his wrist, moving to intertwine with his fingers. "I'm always here if you need me."

He took her into his arms, held her, but for the first time she didn't provide him the comfort he needed. She belonged to his best friend, but more importantly she wasn't Tess.

The blood in his veins froze with the thought. The attraction between them couldn't be denied. Fuck. He'd fallen for Tess and he knew without a doubt it wasn't simply lust. Any other time he would have bed the woman and walked away, but with her it was different.

He jerked his hand out of Jessie's. "I've got to go."

"Clancy?"

"Bye, Jessie." He didn't turn around, just kept on walking toward his truck.

Her steps beat after him. "Clancy? Please. Don't go."

Without pausing he climbed into his truck. She was at his window, her warm palm against the cold glass. He started the engine and she stepped away, leaving a frosty outline of her hand. The sadness in her eyes killed him, but he needed to be alone. Needed to figure out how to get his head screwed on straight, and he couldn't do that here.

He struck out, going north toward Austin when his cell phone rang. For a moment he was a little disoriented. Where was his damn phone? Then he saw it in the dash cubbyhole next to his radio. Grabbing it, he flipped it open.

"Wiseman."

The voice on the other end sounded frantic.

"Milo? Hey, man, slow down."

"I found her."

"Found who?"

"Julie. They're in Amarillo, but someone tipped them off. Debbie is threatening to run. Man. I hate to ask this, but...I-I need money." The man's voice shook. "I've got to get to Amarillo. Stop her."

Clancy slowed his truck, turning onto the shoulder. "Don't worry about the money, Milo." He reversed the vehicle and then headed back the way he came. "Call my attorney, and then the airlines. Book three tickets for Amarillo."

"I can't ask that of you. The lawyer's cost alone will be—"

"Let me worry about that. Call the attorney."

"What if he won't come?"

"He will." Money had a way of swaying people and Clancy would make it right. "I'll swing by the house and pick you up. Throw a couple things in a bag for me. I'll be there in thirty." The phone went dead as he pressed down on the accelerator.

He was there in twenty.

As he drove into the driveway, Milo waited with two bags in hand. His face was flushed, his eyes and nose red. Damn. This was heartbreaking. The man loved his daughter. Why did Debbie see fit to hurt him over and over?

The truck had barely slowed down when Milo reached for the handle. "I can't thank you enough—" He tossed the bags in the backseat, before pinching the bridge of his nose.

"Attorney?"

"He'll meet us at the airport."

"Good. Then there is nothing to worry about. Everything will be okay. Trust me." As the promise slipped from Clancy's lips, he prayed he could live up to it.

Milo needed to be reunited with his daughter.

Chapter Thirteen

Tess's nerves prickled her skin as they grew nearer to the Peterson's ranch. Her hands were sweaty, trembling slightly. It had been over a week since she'd seen or heard from Clancy. According to one of his ranch hands he had gone to Amarillo and wasn't expected back for a while.

As she had left for work Friday, she had seen Clancy's truck pass by her house. Like now, her pulse had sped and her breathing hitched. She didn't know what to expect today, but she had to do what she had to do. Making their ranch a success meant everything, and these were the people who could help her, including Clancy.

Levi's gaze left the road long enough to give her a concerned look. "You okay?"

"Fine. Why?" She wasn't fine, but her brother didn't need to know.

Once again he pulled his attention off the road and glanced down at her fingers thrumming against her thigh. "You're acting nervous."

She curled her fingers into a fist. "There's just so much to learn." And she couldn't forget their finances. Right now they were doing all right, but how long would that last if they had to supplement feed and purchase more stock? But that wasn't the real reason behind her anxiety.

When they approached a gravel road and a large sign that hung above the entrance to the Peterson's homestead, she swallowed, but the knot in her throat refused to dislodge. The words CP Angus Ranch were burned into the largest beam Tess had ever seen. Before her, miles of well-tended white, wooden fences zigzagged along rolling green hills, separating herds of both horses and cattle. She understood immediately the difference between the Peterson's and their own land. Rich green grass flourished, compared to the shorter blades that donned their ground. But this land didn't have their beautiful trees, hilltops or the flowing brooks that cut naturally through the rougher terrain.

Levi let out a low whistle as he slowed the truck, pulling it to a stop, while Tess hopped out to unlock the large wrought iron gate. Giving the heavy gate a push, she walked it back until it was wide enough for her brother to drive through. Then she proceeded to close and refasten the latch, before she climbed back into the vehicle.

Levi's eyes twinkled. "Pretty impressive, huh?"

Yes. It was, but it couldn't hold a candle to Clancy's ranch. The Peterson's ranch home was bigger than theirs, but just as common looking. Not like the elegant home Clancy lived in.

"Look! They're roping." Levi bypassed the house and headed for the arena.

As he maneuvered the truck to a stop, a calf broke from the chute, a horse and rider hot on its heels. The swirling rope above the rider was a work of art. There was almost a musical quality to the flow of the lasso as it soared through the air, before hooking around the animal's neck. The rider nearly flew off his horse. As the Palomino mare began to ease backward, almost dragging the calf, the cowboy ran forward and tossed it on its side. In mere seconds, the calf's legs were tied together. The small crowd watching roared with approval. That's when the man removed his hat.

Oh God. It was Clancy.

Tess hadn't thought she would have to face him today. Well, at least not here at the Peterson's. They weren't scheduled to meet with him until later in the afternoon.

As soon as Shelby saw them, she ran for the truck. Tess barely wedged the door open when the little girl threw her arms around Tess's waist and hugged her.

Tess returned the embrace. "Hi, Shelby."

"Hi, Miss Gilmore. Jessie!" A beautiful, dark-haired woman turned and smiled. "That's my sister. Beside her is Wade, her husband. Ty is his brother."

Oh, Tess knew Ty quite well—maybe too well. He had a freckle on his right ass cheek.

Levi wasted no time joining the men, while Jessie split from them and approached. As her full lips rose into a smile, she held her hand out to greet Tess. "I've heard so much about you."

Unease slithered up Tess's spine as she accepted the woman's hand and shook. "I hope it was good."

Per the gossip, this woman and her husband used to be Clancy's threesome. The thought tightened the tendons in her neck as unease skittered across her skin. A quick assessment found Tess slightly taller. Their hair about the same length, but Jessie's was a midnight-black that shone blue in the sunlight. Athletically built, but curvy in all the right places, the woman was perfect. For some reason that irritated the crap out of Tess.

"Absolutely. All good," she responded.

When a petite blonde joined the men, Wade and Ty both wedged between her and Levi.

Their posturing set Tess's feet in motion. She would make damn sure nothing happened. Because the seductive way the young woman eyed Tess's brother definitely meant trouble and another potential fight for Levi.

Ty walked over to Tess and gave her a big hug, which raised Levi's brows along with Clancy's who had strolled to the fence.

"Tess Gilmore, my brother Wade and my sister Tori. I see you've met our Jessie."

Tess shook Wade's hand. Like Ty, his brother had golden-brown hair and wore a short-cropped mustache and beard. She nodded toward their sister who had taken the opportunity to shake loose of her brothers' protection and now stood next to Levi. When the men realized she'd given them the slip, they both frowned, which rubbed Tess the wrong way. Her brother was a gentleman, a good kid. Yes, he made a mistake that night they had brought him home drunk, but who didn't?

"So, Tori, you go to school with Levi," she asked.

"Yes, ma'am." Even as she answered Tess's question, she batted long eyelashes at Levi.

Tess could have sworn her brother's chest puffed out like a rooster. He tipped back his Stetson and grinned ear to ear. She almost laughed, but knew it wouldn't help matters.

"Levi, come take a look at my new mare." Clancy drew the boy's attention. He climbed through the wooden slats and entered the arena.

Someone tugged at her hand and Tess looked down to see Shelby by her side.

"Tori's teaching me to ride."

"She is?" For the first time since Tess had arrived, she relaxed. Levi was away from Tori. Ty and his brother were no longer scowling. And there was a fence between her and Clancy.

"Our little sister provides riding lessons, not only to adults and children, but she works with the handicapped and less fortunate," Ty said proudly, even as he yanked on one of her braids. She jerked away from him, but not before punching him squarely in the shoulder. "Ouch!" His eyes widened as he rubbed his arm. "See if I ever sing your praises again."

Tori blushed prettily, but clearly her eyes were for Levi who had climbed atop the big yellow horse. She drew closer, gripping the fence and placing a boot on the bottom rung.

"He sits a saddle nicely," she purred. Her brothers didn't miss their sister's interest. Once again they were frowning.

Tess moved beside her. "He's been riding all his life."

"And you?" Ty's sexy voice came from over one of her shoulders.

She didn't turn around, knowing that it would bring them mouth to mouth. Instead her heart leaped in her chest. "When I can." The words came out breathy.

"Good. Riding is the best way to see the ranch. Tori, go saddle two more horses and then you can go inside and help Mom."

"I'm coming with you."

"No!" Wade and Ty spoke in unison, which reminded Tess of her sisters. Given these cowboys' good looks, she was glad that Rose and Rachel had made arrangements to go to the mall with friends today.

"But—"

"Tori." The firmness in Wade's tone must have clinched the deal, because his sister released a *harrumph*. "Come on, Shelby. You can help me."

As the sound of gravel popping beneath feet drifted away, Jessie joined Tess at the fence. "We're having a couple friends over for a barbeque at lunch time. I hope you'll join us."

"Thank you, but—"

"She'd love to." Ty hovered over her. Way too close for comfort.

"Ty, back off and give the woman some breathing room." Jessie smiled knowingly. "The Petersons have a way of making it hard for a woman to think."

Shit. Shit. Shit.

Tess got the distinct feeling this woman knew about her and Ty, but did she know about Clancy too?

Wade circled his arms around his wife's waist, pulling her back against his chest. "And I like my woman that way." Jessie giggled, before she turned her head to receive her husband's kiss.

Their show of affection tightened Tess's chest.

Would she ever have a relationship like theirs? Even with Ty so near, she glanced at Clancy, who stood looking up at her brother still perched high atop the horse. She couldn't hear what they were saying, but Levi nodded and climbed off the horse.

"Clancy's good with children," Jessie offered. "He'll make a fine husband some day."

Tess snapped her head around in disbelief. The woman grinned.

She knew—she knew about the three of them.

Wrapped in Wade's arms, Jessie deepened her smile. "Clancy hasn't said a word to you since you arrived." She didn't elaborate further. Her husband kept his gaze forward, but Tess could see him fighting a grin of his own.

They all knew.

"Awkward." Ty chuckled behind her and she wanted to strangle the scoundrel.

Awkward didn't begin to describe the moment. She was beyond embarrassed. Lord help her. She prayed that Tori wasn't aware of her indiscretion. She would die if Levi ever discovered the truth, and then there were her sisters. While Tess died a little inside, Clancy and Levi joined them.

Wade released his hold on Jessie. "Let's saddle up." As she started to walk away, he struck her playfully on the ass. She startled. Frowning, she looked over a shoulder, but there was no malice in her eyes, only love.

"She isn't going with us?" Tess asked.

"Nah. She's helping Mom and Tori with the preparations for the barbeque."

As they headed toward the line of horses tied to a hitching post outside the barn, Wade began to explain the workings of their ranch. "Clint, our eldest brother, works more with our dad and the finances. They had to go to town this morning, but I'm sure one of them will be happy to speak with you during the barbeque."

One thing Tess knew for sure was they would *not* be staying for the party.

If Ty accidently rubbed against Tess's arm one more time, Clancy swore he would kill the man. As he watched the couple about thirty feet away, heat built beneath the collar of his plaid western shirt, shooting sparks of jealousy up his neck. Ty's attention made her squirm where she sat at a picnic table. Several times she had discreetly removed his arm from around her shoulders, but that was Ty. The cowboy was a rogue to the nth degree.

He tried to ignore them. Tried to keep his mind off the woman who had preoccupied his thoughts while he tended to things in Amarillo.

For the time being, Milo had custody of Julie. It didn't help his ex's cause when she threatened to take the child out of the country in front of the judge. Clancy had testified that Milo had the means and home to take care of Julie, which meant he'd moved them both into the main house. It would be that way until other arrangements could be made. In all honesty, there was something nice about having a child in the house.

"Move over." Jessie took a seat next to him on a picnic bench. She remained silent, only the music of a four-piece country western band played while his head spun with the events of the last week.

"So are you going to just sit here and stare at her or are you going to make your move?" Jessie was never good at beating around the bush.

Clancy glanced down at the half-eaten corncob sitting on his plate. "I don't know what you're talking about." He picked up his fork and chased a pork and bean around the succulent beef he had yet to try, the rich brown-sugar scent filling his nose.

"Bullshit." She choked, and then she laughed. "Clancy. Clancy. Clancy. When will you learn not to lie to me? Who knows you better than me?"

Setting his fork down, he raised his head so that their eyes met. "No one." She knew him almost as well as he knew himself.

"Exactly." She paused, her voice softening. "You only pull away from people you care about. The second you get interested in a woman you haul ass." He followed her line of sight, which led straight to Tess. "And you're interested or you wouldn't be trying to ignore her so thoroughly. She's nice. Intelligent. Beautiful. Did I say nice?"

"Yeah. So?" There was no use in denying it. He tugged his Stetson a little lower over his eyes.

"Have you noticed how she looks at you when she doesn't think you're aware?"

No he hadn't, because he'd been too busy trying to ignore her. "That doesn't change the circumstances."

"And exactly what are those circumstances?" Her voice grew taut.

"You know damn well what they are."

Jessie released a pent-up breath. "You are hardheaded. That was your dad's—your family's—history, not yours. Clancy, when are you going to pull your head out of your ass and realize that you're a good man—a gentle man? A man who deserves to love and be loved in return." She shot off the bench. "You know, screw this. Let the best thing that has walked into your life pass you by." Then an expression of regret fell across her face. "I'm sorry." She hugged his neck. "I just worry about you."

"You don't have to worry about me." He patted her arm. "I'm happy, Jessie."

Broken laughter spilled from her lips as she released him and flicked the brim of his hat with her fingers. "Sure you are, buddy. About as happy as I was before Wade forced me to wake up and smell the roses. Don't forget to whom you're talking to. Remember we were cut from the same piece of cloth. I know what you're thinking, but you'd never hurt a woman, especially one you cared about. So get off your ass and go claim what you want, before Ty sweet talks her away."

"Jessie, you don't understand." No one understood the demons inside him.

She squeezed his arm. "I understand a helluva lot more than you think. But if you're all right with Ty sweeping her off her feet and maybe eliciting Guy Sandoval to take your place in a threesome, so be it."

Guy Sandoval? A friend and attorney for the Peterson family and a Spanish Casanova who had cut a path through more women than even Clancy had thought about?

No fuckin' way. A growl rumbled deep in his throat.

When he raised his gaze to meet Jessie's, she wore a shit-eating grin. "Just what I thought," she purred with delight. "You don't want Guy touching your woman, much less Ty. Am I right? Tell me I'm wrong."

"You know, Jessie, sometimes you can be a little bitch."

"Yeah, but you still love me." She planted a kiss on his cheek. "Now stop brooding and let Tess know how you feel about her."

"Hmmm. No can do. She's already made it clear that she doesn't need a cowboy like me to muddy her reputation." And who could blame her?

"Really, Clancy?" Jessie released a heavy breath. "I've seen you charm the pants off the most frigid of cowgirls, so don't tell me this is different."

But it was different. Tess was different. And his emotions were different.

"Ohhhh... Lookie," Jessie cooed.

Clancy once again followed her line of sight. Ty and Tess were rising from where they sat.

"If I know Ty, he's attempting to get her into the barn. Alone." Jessie let an ominous note hang on her last word. "You remember that barn, don't you, Clancy? All those stalls a couple could get lost in."

"It won't work, Jessie. I'm not jealous." The hell he wasn't. Just the thought of Tess in Ty's arms sent an army of fire ants stinging their way over his skin. He twitched, but didn't get up.

"Oh. Okay." Her eyes widened with false belief that he knew hid behind those scheming, blue eyes. "I guess I'll join my husband. Maybe make him take me for a spin across the dance floor." She waved her fingers at Clancy. "Have fun." And then she was gone.

Thankfully, the barn hadn't been what Ty had in mind. No, the damn cowboy had chosen just the right slow dance to get Tess in his arms.

Begrudgingly, Clancy watched them. Sometime between the beginning and middle of the song, Clancy realized she had danced away with his heart. He wanted this woman. Getting to his feet, he moved closer. By the time the song ended, he was near enough to tap Ty on the shoulder, but it wasn't to be.

Tori and a handful of her girlfriends raced up to Tess. "Shelby says you're the choirmaster at her school. Will you sing for us? Please."

Tess's cheeks reddened. "I shouldn't—can't. I mean—"

"Please." Tori's friends joined her pleas.

"I'd like to hear you sing." Clancy caught Tess's attention, swearing he could hear her heart beating rapidly, but it was his own. She did this to him.

"Okay," she whispered.

Tori and her friends squealed, as she grabbed Tess's hand and led her to where the band was. The lead singer of the group was Austin Anderson. He spoke briefly with Tess and then he nodded at his keyboard player. The tinkling of the ivory keys joined by the drummer, and then the guitarist, announced the song was Lady Antebellum's *Need You Now*.

The first line of the song came out of Tess's mouth as smooth as Tennessee whiskey. He had never heard a voice so beautiful, so arousing. When she sang the lyrics about her ever crossing his mind, she looked right at him, setting his pulse racing.

When Austin joined her in the chorus, she turned toward him. The man's rich voice complemented hers as if they had been singing together for a lifetime. But it was her tone, the way her body swayed to the music, that captivated Clancy. Each tender expression threw a net over the audience, reeling them in hook, line and sinker. They were spellbound and that included Clancy.

By the time the music died, he felt like one big knot of emotion. Jessie was right. He'd never felt this way about a woman. Yet he had known that from the second he had looked into Tess's eyes that rainy night—he would never be the same.

She was an angel—his angel—and he needed her more than he needed to breathe. Which wasn't all that easy when a herd of cowboys stampeded her direction.

"What the hell?" he grumbled, making his way through the crowd. As he neared, her laughter stroked his ears. "Levi wants to see you." He grabbed her hand and quickly maneuvered her away from the fold.

"Is he okay?" Concern darkened her eyes, her footsteps hastening.

Clancy nodded in the direction where Levi stood surrounded by at least five teenage girls. "He's more than okay." The young buck glanced at them, grinning like a fool.

She twisted her head, continuing to watch her brother as they passed by him. "Is he ready to go?"

"No." Clancy guided her farther away from the throng.

"If he wanted me, why are we going the opposite direction?"

As Clancy whisked her through the open barn door, he announced, "Because I lied."

"Lied? I don't understand."

Maybe she would understand this. Clancy pressed her against the wall, his body covering hers, before he captured her mouth with an urgency he couldn't control.

She released a small cry of surprise, but her lips softened against his, parting when he nudged the seam with his tongue. Hands trembling, he cupped the nape of her neck and angled his head to deepen the kiss, devouring her mouth like a starving man. When he released her to take a breath, she whimpered with something close to disappointment.

"I want you," he groaned.

She put her lips to his mouth and murmured, "We can't." Even as she spoke, she tugged his shirttail up, caressing her hands beneath the long-sleeved cotton shirt. Her warm touch sent a million chills across his pebbling skin, alerting his senses. He could hear her labored breathing. Smell her sweet perfume mixing with the aroma of horses, hay and oats.

He pressed his forehead to hers. "Darlin', you're saying one thing, while your hands are speaking a completely different language."

Tess froze. Her fingers curled into fists against his back. "It doesn't matter what I want. We can't do this ever again."

"Don't tell me it doesn't matter, because it matters to me. Do you have any idea what it's like to be around you and not touch you? It's killing me." He shook with the declaration, leaving him feeling raw and exposed.

"I want you too, but—" She wet her lips. "Maybe we could— " she swallowed hard before continuing, "—keep this thing between us quiet."

Every muscle and tendon in his body stiffened. Any other time her suggestion would be exactly what Clancy desired. But this was a huge leap of faith he was taking. He was putting himself out there and he needed the same commitment from her.

"I don't want to be your dirty, little secret. Nor do I want to share you. Tess, I want to see where this thing between us leads, but either we're in a relationship or we're not. You can't have it both ways. It's your choice."

Chapter Fourteen

Her dirty, little secret?

At the time Tess made the hasty suggestion to continue their affair, but keep it on the down low, she hadn't realized how obtuse it had sounded. Hell. If she had been in Clancy's place, she'd have been insulted, even pissed. Instead he looked crestfallen, hurt.

"I'm so sorry." She flattened her fisted hands on his back, loving the feel of his skin beneath her palms, as she pulled him closer. "It's just that my decisions are not my own. They affect my family."

He dipped a finger beneath her chin, forcing her to meet his gaze. "I know I'm not the kind of man you envisioned in your life, but I won't sulk in the shadows—"

Even for you, she heard his unspoken words. When he stepped out of her arms, she knew he had meant what he had said earlier. She couldn't have it both ways, and who could blame him? Not her.

Still, she had to make him understand. "It's complicated—"

"Dammit, Tess." He whipped off his hat and brushed his hand over his head. "Don't you think I know it's complicated? No one knows complicated like me." His eyes hardened. "I don't want to just fuck you. I want to see where this *thing* between us is going."

"I'm sorry," she murmured again, feeling her heart sink.

He sat his hat back on his head, tugging the rim low over his eyes. "We better get back to the crowd before someone realizes you're with me." She flinched at the coldness in his tone as he tucked his shirttails in his jeans. His expression wasn't much better when he pivoted. Before she could say anything, he slipped through the door, leaving her behind.

Tess half expected Clancy to not be outside, waiting, when she exited. But he leaned against the side of the barn, pushing away from it when she stepped beside him. In silence they walked back toward the party.

Shelby ran up to Tess, out of breath. "Miss Gilmore," she gasped. "I've been looking for you."

Clancy paused, a chill rolling off him that Tess felt bone deep. "Perhaps tomorrow would be a better day to tour my ranch. Say about ten." He didn't wait for an answer. Instead he tipped his hat and walked away.

Only when Shelby began to speak again, did Tess tear her gaze off of him. "Tori said the band wants you to sing with them again."

"Ah, honey, I'm not in the mood."

Tess glanced over the child's head to see Clancy join a group of cowboys tapping off a beer keg. A tall, slender man slapped him on the back, before handing him a plastic cup half filled with foam. When a petite, dark-haired woman flung her arms around Clancy's neck, hugging him, Tess's breath caught.

"B-besides, it's time for us to leave." She had to get out of there.

"Leave?" Jessie approached from behind them. "You can't leave now. The party is just getting started."

Tears beckoned, but Tess held on to them. "My sisters should be getting home soon. I need to cook supper. Feed the stock." *Throw myself on top of my bed and cry my eyes out, because I let the only man I've ever wanted slip through my fingers.*

"We can send some of the boys to feed the stock and pick up the girls. As you can see, we didn't make a dent in the food."

153

Sure enough, a good portion of the slab of beef still remained rotating slowly on the spit over a dying fire.

When Tess saw the woman who hung on Clancy drag him out on the makeshift dance floor, Tess gasped, and then she cursed her inability to hold on to her control.

Jessie frowned, her voice lowering. "Shelby, go fetch Miss Gilmore's brother." Her concern bled through, but she didn't comment. As her sister ran off, she linked her arm through Tess's and cast her a wary smile. "Madeline, Wade's mother, made her famous strawberry-rhubarb pie. It's to die for."

"But—"

"It won't do you any good to argue with her." Wade sat alone atop a picnic table nursing a glass of whiskey. The ice clinked against the sides as he sat it down. Then the handsome cowboy winked at his wife. "I learned a long time ago just to give her what she wants."

"*Pshhh.*" Jessie brushed him off with a hand through the air. "Ignore the silly man. I think a little girl talk is in order."

Oh God no. The last thing Tess wanted to do was talk. "Thank you for the invitation, but we really should go." The words came out a little desperate.

Shelby came skipping up to them.

Tess scanned the horizon for her brother. "Where's Levi?"

"He left."

"Left?" A wave of panic tightened her throat and threatened to squeeze the air out of her lungs.

"Yep. Said he'd feed the stock, pick up Rose and Rachel and bring them back to the party."

If Jessie noticed Tess's inability to breathe she didn't let on. Instead, she squeezed Tess's arm. "There. Everything is settled. Why don't we find a nice quiet spot and chat. Wade, how about grabbing us a couple of drinks? Beer okay with you?"

Tess quietly nodded, while the sensation of being trapped closed in on her. It seemed the entire world was conspiring against her. She tried not to look at the dance floor, but the need was like a drug in her system pulling her gaze toward it.

Clancy and the woman in his arms moved as if they were one. Each step and executed turn one of precision, as if they knew what move the next one would take before it happened. When he smiled down upon the rare beauty, Tess died a little more inside.

Jessie steered her away, forcing Tess to take her eyes off of the couple. "You know, sometimes the things we think aren't good for us are exactly what we need." She stopped beneath a large oak tree, where a white wrought iron table and two chairs sat. "Have a seat." Releasing Tess's arm, she pulled out a chair and sat down. "You know he's a good man."

Tess didn't pretend to not know whom she referred to, choosing instead not to respond.

"His life hasn't been easy." Jessie hesitated as if she sought the right words. "He'd kill me if he knew I was divulging his secrets, but he cares for you and I would hate to see him screw this up."

Ironic laughter spilled for Tess's lips earning her a frown from the woman sitting across from her. "It's not him. It's me. My situation. Since my parents died, I have guardianship of my brother and sisters. My choices aren't my own. I have to protect them. My job."

"I see. How old are your sisters?"

"Fifteen going on thirty."

Jessie chuckled. "Sounds like Shelby. But what about you? What do you want? Need?"

Clancy's name whispered through her head. "What I want or need doesn't matter. I have to do what is good for my family."

"And Clancy's notorious reputation isn't." It wasn't a question, but a statement. Jessie leaned back in her seat. "Well, if you've heard those rumors, then I'm sure you know about Clancy, me and Wade."

With the mention of her husband's name he approached with two beers in hand. Without a word, he set the drinks down, kissed Jessie softly on the cheek, and then he turned and walked away.

Jessie picked up her beer and took a sip. "Funny how preconceived notions of right and wrong screw with our lives. Honestly, I can't say I regret anything between us." She looked away wistfully, tipping the cup up to her mouth again. "The ol' hussies around here will talk, gossip, but in the end it has to be your decision. I can't tell you what is right for you, but I can say that Clancy is worth fighting for. You won't find a more caring, loving man. Even if he doesn't see himself in that light. Did you know he donated all the playground equipment at Shelby's school? What kind of man does that?" She paused, her hard gaze fixed on Tess. "He needs a woman like you to complete him. To show him he's a man worthy of love."

This wasn't helping. In fact, it made Tess feel worse. She had seen the shadows in his eyes. Felt him pull away and then back again, as if he struggled with something darker.

Like a glutton for punishment, she slid her gaze toward the dance floor just as the music stopped. Her throat tightened when the dark-haired woman went on her tiptoes, throwing her arms around Clancy's neck. She pulled him down to her and the air in Tess's chest seized. Her pulse sped, heart pounding.

Please, don't kiss her. Even as the thought invaded her mind she chastised herself. She had no right—

"You're the only woman Clancy has ever wanted to get close to."

"What?" Tess snapped her head toward Jessie, choking "Me?" before her riveted gaze returned to the dance floor just in time to see the dark-haired beauty's lips touch Clancy's.

The sudden onslaught of emotions left Tess feeling like a leaf in a windstorm being tossed asunder. She couldn't breathe, not until he jerked back and put some distance between him and the woman's plump, red lips. But the hussy only laughed, looking up through sultry, long lashes, as she dragged a long fingernail down his chest.

"See?" Jessie hummed behind Tess, sending chills up her spine. "You confuse him. Thrill him. You make him forget himself. But I see the longing in his eyes for love. A family. You."

"It's not that easy." Nothing was easy. With a knot in her throat, Tess watched the woman standing before Clancy lean into him, her sexy body rubbing against his.

"It's not supposed to be. You have to fight for what you want. Do you want him?"

"Yes," she hissed, before she realized it.

"Then let him know before he makes a mistake. Becky won't stop until she's in his bed tonight. Is that what you want?"

Without further thought, Tess got to her feet.

"Not tonight." As they stood in the middle of the empty makeshift dance floor, Clancy attempted one more time to discreetly break Rebecca Allen's hold, but she was having none of it and clung to his waist.

"Please." She looked up at him through lowered lashes.

He had to give it to the sexy brunette. She was persistent. But going home with her tonight or even slipping into the barn for a quickie as she had suggested earlier just didn't interest him. Only one woman was on his mind, and if he couldn't have Tess tonight—he didn't want anyone.

"Clancy?" When he heard her sweet voice, he thought he imagined it. But when he glanced over his shoulder, Tess stood behind him. Her eyes never left his as she stepped even closer. "You promised me a dance."

Becky cleared her throat. Cocking a brow, her grasp on him tightened. She dragged a slow, indifferent gaze over Tess, who returned one of her own that shocked the living hell out of him.

Tess couldn't be jealous. Still, the thought sent warmth through his veins that heated his body. He parted his lips to make introductions when Jessie sauntered up.

"Becky." She wedged herself between the brunette and Clancy, forcing her to release him. "I've been looking all over for you. Any chance you'd help me bring out the desserts?"

"I— Clancy— I mean, *we* were just thinking of leaving." She stared helplessly at Clancy, but she was on her own.

"Nonsense. You can't leave now." Jessie scooped Becky's hand in hers. "C'mon. I heard Wade's mother made her special pie." With a tug, she led the reluctant woman away, but not before they both looked back.

Becky frowned. Jessie winked.

Clancy slid his gaze to Tess. "What was that about?"

"I..." she shifted nervously, "made a mistake earlier."

"Mistake?"

"I want to see where this thing between us leads."

His chest thickened with emotion, and he was afraid to believe what he was hearing. "You realize what you're saying?"

She released an uneasy chuckle. "Not really. But I'm willing to give it a try."

In front of everyone he pulled her into his arms. His heart skipped a beat when she went willingly. As he lost himself in the depth of her blue eyes, the band struck up another tune and people began to join them on the dance floor. There was so much they needed to talk about. Then someone bumped into him.

"See, the way this thing called dancing works is that you move your feet and the lovely lady follows." Ty tipped his hat as he flashed Tess a roguish grin. "Let me show you how it's done." He reached for her, but Clancy eased them around so that his body blocked the man's grasp.

"I think I can handle this by myself." The note of possessiveness in his voice didn't escape him as well as his friend.

Ty placed a palm over his heart. His expression fell, but the twinkle in his eyes gave him away. "I'm hurt." He paused for a moment, but Clancy knew it was only for effect. Then the cowboy leaned in to Tess and whispered, "It sounds as if our brief threesome has become a twosome."

"You heard right." Clancy released Tess long enough to gather her hand in his. "C'mon. We're getting out of here." He couldn't wait to taste her lips, hold her in his arms unrestricted from wandering eyes.

"I can't." She quickly scanned the crowd, locating her siblings who had just arrived. "I can't leave them behind."

"Levi can drive them home."

"But—"

"You can call them from the truck."

"Where are we going?"

"Home." Damn. His footsteps faltered. He couldn't take a woman to his house. Not with a child just down the hall.

"What's wrong?"

"Julie."

Tess's eyes widened. "Julie?"

"Now, darlin', it's not what you think." He gave her hand a squeeze and urged her forward. "Julie is Milo's daughter. The courts gave him temporary custody and he needed a place for them to stay. I couldn't let the child sleep in the bunkhouse with the rest of the hands, so they moved into my house until he finds other lodgings and daycare."

"Milo is a friend of yours?"

"He works for me." Clancy unlocked his truck and opened the passenger-side door, stepping aside.

Tess climbed in. "Where's her mother?"

He didn't answer her immediately. Instead he hurried around the vehicle and slid behind the wheel. "Last I saw she was slinging insults, accusations and threats in Amarillo." With a twist of the key, the engine roared to life.

"So this is a good thing?"

"Milo's a good man. Loves his daughter. God help him, I think he still loves his wife." Ranching and being faithful to one man wasn't what Debbie envisioned. She had bigger plans. Plans that had included charming Clancy, but he had been quick to set her straight. His only regret was that Milo had been blind to her promiscuous ways. "She took every penny he had and ran off with their two-year-old daughter. He's been looking for them for six months. When we found them, Debbie was out of work, living in a broken-down travel trailer with no air conditioning. Nearly broke Milo's heart."

He fought the anger that resurfaced as he remembered the day they had walked into that sordid neighborhood and found the child. Julie had been hungry, dirty and unkempt. Her beautiful brown hair a nest of knots. But the smile she gave Milo when she saw him had melted Clancy's heart. What he would give to have a child of his own look at him that way.

"So you helped him?"

Clancy shrugged. "For right now, the two of us will take care of Julie." What else could he do? He would make damn sure Milo had what he needed to raise Julie the right way.

When Tess touched his thigh, he turned toward her. "Why don't we go to my house? Levi and the girls won't be home for a while."

The tenderness in the way she looked at him made his chest tighten. "You sure?"

She smiled softly. "Absolutely."

For the rest of the drive, a comfortable silence filled the space between them, something that had never happened with another woman. Instead, anticipation prickled across his skin, stirred his blood. He couldn't wait to make love to Tess, this time with no third-party intervention. The thought made his cock tighten. By the time he maneuvered his truck in front of her house and eased to a stop, a full-blown hard-on pressed against his jeans.

He glanced at her and she returned his heated gaze. Without words, both of them reached for the door handle at the same time. The second they were outside, facing each other, he pulled her into his arms. Warm and willing, she softened against him, her arms snaking around his neck. Flutters erupted low in his belly, and he was achingly aware of every inch of her beautiful body. He smoothed a palm down her back, pausing just above her ass to ease her closer and inhale the sweet fragrance that was uniquely Tess.

She felt so right, so perfect.

"Kiss me," she whispered in his ear, setting his heart to pound.

A groan rose in his throat. He tilted his head and sealed his mouth over hers in a gentle caress. When he nudged the seam of her lips, she parted them, sighing, as he dipped inside.

Good God. She tasted like heaven.

For a few seconds more, he reveled in her moist heat, drinking in her essence. When the kiss erupted into a burning passion, he couldn't restrain another growl from erupting. He cupped the mounds of her ass, lifting her off her feet, needing to get closer.

"I want you. Now."

She locked her ankles around his waist. "Let's go inside."

With hastened steps, he carried her to the front door, then released her so that she slid slowly down his body, rubbing against his throbbing arousal. As he gazed down upon her, her lips were a temptation he couldn't pass up. She met him halfway, their mouths fusing together, nearly knocking off his hat in the process.

"Damn, darlin'," was all he could say as he leaned in for one more kiss.

"Key," she moaned.

"What?" He nibbled on her bottom lip and she mewled.

"I need to get the key." Stepping out of his arms, she moved toward a potted plant sitting on the porch, tipped it slightly, and retrieved the key beneath. She barely got the door open before he slid past her, grabbing her hand to lead her inside and back into his embrace. As the door closed behind them, he blanketed her mouth with his.

Lord, what was wrong with him?

He couldn't stand to let her go for even a moment. Something in his head registered that this hold she had on him wasn't good, but then she stroked his tongue with lush slides of her own before trapping him in her mouth and sucking with gentle pulls. That's when all rational thought disappeared.

Chapter Fifteen

Tess fell into Clancy's embrace, feeling every hot, hard inch of his body against hers. She hungered for his kiss, his touch. When their mouths met in a blaze of fiery heat, the key slipped, pinging against the wooden floor. Her fingers curled into the front of his shirt.

The fervor of his caresses stole her breath, made her mind spin as her breasts became heavy with desire. When he shoved his hands beneath her shirt, skin stroking skin, a sting radiated through each nipple, spreading like wildfire throughout her tender globes. As his palms moved upward to skim the underside of her bra, her knees weakened, moisture pooling between her thighs.

Yes. This is what she longed for—needed.

The click of the door shutting startled her back to reality. She jerked away, only to discover he had given the door a kick to close them off from the rest of the world.

"Sorry." His mouth curved into a slow, heart-stopping smile that melted her heart. Without pause, she returned to where she belonged—in his arms.

His warm breath danced across her skin as he strung kisses down her throat to the hollow of a shoulder blade. "Too many clothes." When he glanced up at her, his gaze darkened and his voice lowered to a rough timbre. "I need you naked."

His sensual command and the heady pheromones he emitted made her giddy, high on what the night promised. A surge of arousal tightened the flesh between her legs, forcing her eyes closed. But a cool breeze from her shirt rising swept across her abdomen and encouraged her heavy eyelids to flicker open. The intent expression on Clancy's face as he eased her shirt farther up and over her head before he tossed the garment aside, sent her heart racing.

For a moment he only stared at her exposed flesh as if in awe. Then he moaned, "You're so beautiful."

He made her feel beautiful and needy. Without hesitation, she reached behind her and unfastened her bra. Shrugging out of the satin and lace, she watched as his eyes darkened even more.

"Now you." She dragged her gaze slowly up his rock-hard body, until their eyes met again in a heated exchange.

His black Stetson was the first to go as he set it on the credenza against the wall. It looked like his hands trembled as his fingers fumbled with the buttons of his cotton cowboy shirt. Never once did he draw his eyes off of hers. She wanted him so badly that she reached out to finish the task. Pushing the shirt from his broad shoulders, she exposed an impressive chest, bulging biceps and sexy jeans slung low around his hips. Then he slid his tongue between his lips in an action so sensual her heart thudded.

What was it about him that made her breathless, made her want to throw caution to the wind? To take a calculated risk on a man who could ruin her reputation, and worse, break her heart if he walked away?

"I love it when you look at me that way," he said.

"What way—" Her breath caught as he caressed her cheek with his knuckles.

"Like you want to eat me."

Tess couldn't help it, her gaze dropped to the bulge in his jeans and her mouth began to salivate. She reached for him, tucked her fingertips in the front of his waistband and pulled him to her. He moved the small distance between them willingly. A heartbeat passed before she began to unfasten his buckle, belt and then the button. As she tugged on his zipper, the metal hissed, heating her blood.

God, this sexy cowboy did it for her—made her horny as hell.

Hooking her thumbs on each side of his pants and skivvies, she inched them down, exposing him, as she dropped to her jeans-covered knees in the process.

"I can't lie." She smiled up to him. "Eating you sounds delicious."

Dragging her fingernails up his muscular thighs, she took his hand in hers to guide his middle finger into her mouth. As she suckled, easing the digit in and out, she moaned, thinking of their bodies intimately connected. Cheeks hollow, she made a popping sound as she released his finger.

"Mmmm..." Tess hummed and closed her hand firmly around his cock. She stroked once, twice, and then twisted gently.

He inhaled sharply, but didn't say a word. Instead there was a dangerous growl to his voice as he stabbed his fingers through her hair, urging her head and mouth closer.

Something about the way he took control made her pulse beat faster. Breathless, she let him guide her until the bulbous head of his erection rested against her lips. Through feathered lashes, she looked up again. "I can't wait to taste you."

His nostrils flared and that sandpapery rumble erupted in his throat again. His grasp on her hair tightened and he pulled with enough aggression to stroke the flame burning inside her.

Inhaling, she dragged his earthy scent deep into her lungs, and then her lips parted and she licked a leisurely path from root to tip. All she could think of was velvet over steel.

His pupils dilated as he watched his cock slide into her warm and anxious mouth. A stream of air hissed from between his clenched teeth and he grew impossibly harder, longer.

"Ahhh...muhhh...gawwdd."

His nearly unintelligible words shot a thrill from her mouth to her nipples to her pussy. She clenched her thighs together, attempting to ward off the edginess developing. Instead she turned her attention to the heavy veins that coursed his length. Flattening her tongue along them, she paid homage to those areas that elicited a slight quiver and groan from him. Then with long, lavish licks, she caressed the underside of the crest of his erection. A strangled sound rose in his throat that made a smile tease the corner of her mouth.

And then it hit her.

This cowboy could have anyone he wanted and he wanted her. Not to share like his other affairs, but for his very own. The thought fueled her excitement, sending chills up her spine. She inhaled through her nose and his musk filled her senses, clouding her thoughts.

A flick of her tongue over the small slit and the taste of his salty sweet fluid made her want even more. Working her mouth down him, she lightly scraped her teeth along his shaft, licking and sucking the sensitive membrane of his frenulum. Then she placed a kiss upon the top.

His head fell back as his breathing hitched. "Damn, woman." It took several seconds for him to inhale again. Then he leveled his hot gaze on her. "Fuck me, baby. Deep. Hard."

Hair tangled in his fingers, he drew her head back and drove his hips once again against her lips. He slid so far into her mouth that she almost choked, but recovered quickly. Once again she focused on breathing through her nose. As her saliva gathered in her mouth, she swallowed around him. The throaty sounds he released urged her onward.

As her head bobbed, she guided her hand up and down his cock, squeezing and releasing, while she cupped his balls with her other hand. They were heavy and big in her palm, drawing up as she tickled and rolled them between her fingers.

"Tess." His voice was a guttural rasp. She was determined to bring him to climax, sliding her mouth up and down him, but he had other thoughts when he groaned, "God. Stop."

She whimpered around his cock, too far gone to heed his plea.

What she wanted—craved—to hear was him shattering, coming apart and losing that control he seemed to cherish so much. Just the thought of rendering him mindless sent white lightning surging through her veins.

She grasped his thighs, her greedy mouth and tongue clinging, enjoying every gasp and jerk he made. Only the bittersweet pain throbbing at the roots of her hair as he forced her head farther back awoke her from the depths of ecstasy that had its hold on her.

His grip loosened. "Baby." He dragged air into his lungs like it was the most difficult thing to do, before he released it slowly and continued to speak. "Come here."

Helping her to stand on rubbery legs, he supported her by pulling her into his embrace. Their mouths were so close. When they fused together, he kissed her as if she were the only woman on this earth. Lips so soft—yet firm. His mouth devoured her as his tongue left no place untouched.

Tess gave back with a hunger to match his. Her tongue slipped into his mouth. Tasted. Captured the moan that rose in the back of his throat.

When they parted on a gasp, he rubbed his stubbled cheek against hers. "I want to fuck you until you can't breathe. Until you feel me on every inch of your body—inside and out."

The resolution in his voice made her tremble. With each inhale and exhale, her nipples rasped his chest and set her heartbeat to drum in her ears. She couldn't wait—didn't want to wait.

"Promise," she hissed.

"Yes." *Fuck. Yes.*

The burning desire in her eyes nearly undid Clancy. His cock thrust eagerly against her hip, aching with the need to be buried deep inside her. He started to shuffle them toward the couch, but his jeans wrapped around ankles stopped him. He cursed, glancing down at his feet.

She giggled, the soft sound so innocent and sweet it squeezed his chest. He released her. "How 'bout I take these damn things off and you do the same?" He didn't have to ask her twice. While she undressed, he fished a condom out of his pocket and donned it.

Within seconds she stood before him as naked as he. Once again he found himself spellbound, unable to touch her. She was perfection. Too good for the likes of him.

"Are you sure?" His jaws tightened.

She cocked a brow, and then placed a warm palm against his chest. With her sight locked on his, she took a step forward, pushing him backward until the back of his knees struck the couch. Then she gave him a shove. He fell upon the soft cushion. Without speaking, she straddled him, lowering herself so that her moist heat cradled him.

"Does this answer your question?"

Blood rushed to his groin, forcing his teeth together. He couldn't have responded even if he wanted to.

As she leaned in to him, he fought to calm his arousal. When her mouth closed on his throat and she sucked, long and hard, he had no doubt she left her mark on him. The thought elicited a groan from him. Then her teeth scored him, the sharp nip playful and seductive at the same time. A burst of pleasure filled his veins and coursed through his body. He raised his hips and she began to rock against him.

Her hot core caressed and teased him to the point he couldn't hold back. He grasped her hips and raised her. Controlling her movements, he rubbed her clit across his dick once, twice. Her ragged moan urged him to do it one more time before he eased her down upon his shaft. Inch by delicious inch, he pushed into her tight, wet pussy, until he was seated deep inside.

He slowly lifted her, feeling her glide like silk over him. As he eased her back down, he held his breath. Damn. He had never felt anything so fuckin' good. He repeated the process, again and again. When her fingernails dug into his shoulders and her pupils darkened, he held their bodies together and rotated his hips. Her lips parted on a cry. Her breathing was short, airy pants, and then her inner muscles clamped down on him and squeezed.

From out of nowhere a tremor raced up his spine like a high-speed elevator going upward at the same time a blissful sensation released a wave of pleasure that built at the base of his penis. The head of his cock became so sensitive he nearly lost it a couple of times.

Holding on by the skin of his teeth, he sought the bundle of nerves between her thighs. He stroked, moving his fingers in a light circular motion that made her gasp.

A flush of color spread across her cheeks. "Clancy!" Her hips moved wildly against him. Her breathing more pronounced.

He kept thrusting. Faster. Harder.

Her thighs tightened around his. "Oh." Her body shivered. "God. Clancy. Oh Clancy." A deep, wrenching moan followed her cries as pleasure washed over her.

As he watched a multitude of emotions ripple across her beautiful face, his own release rose like an imminent wave, nearly blinding him and throwing him into a world of sensations. His butt cheeks clenched, his anus clamped up, as a surge of electricity shot from his ass to his dick. The overwhelming pull gripped, contorted and twisted everything from his head to his toes. As his cock jerked and his seed burst free, an unexplainable energy coursed through him, leaving him feeling more sated then he had ever felt before.

She dissolved against his moist chest. Their flesh was slick and clammy. He rested his forehead in the curve of her neck, attempting to regulate his breathing, but she had done a job on him. Clancy knew he'd never be the same.

For several minutes they simply held each other. No one spoke. No one moved. When the coolness of the night swept over them and she shivered, he raised his head, holding her at arm's length. Her rosy nipples beaded, small rises pimpled across her areolas, inviting him to warm them up.

"Cold?" He ran his palms up and down her bare arms, feeling her pebbling goose bumps. "If I had you at my place, you'd be buried beneath a mound of blankets. The least I can do is start a fire." He glanced over at the hearth, dreading the knowledge he'd have to release her to do so.

"I—"

He didn't like the concern waging in her eyes. "What?"

"As much as I'd like to continue this upstairs, I'm not sure when Levi and the girls will get home once they discover I've left the barbeque. I'd hate for them to find us in a compromising position."

Damn. He'd forgotten all about her siblings, but she was right.

She placed her palms on each side of his neck, a smile twinkling in her eyes.

"What?"

She bit the right side of her bottom lip, fighting a grin. "Sorry," she chuckled.

"Sorry? For what?"

"Uhm... I left a hickey."

He glowed inside like a damn fool. "I'll wear your mark proudly."

"It's not small. And—" She bit her bottom lip, again fighting a grin. "It's already purple."

"I wouldn't have it any other way." He pulled her to him. "Maybe I should return the favor."

Tess laughed. "You can't." She struggled when he attempted to kiss her neck, but he held her tightly. When his mouth found the tender skin of her throat, she shrieked, "*No! What would I say to the girls? Levi? My class?*"

"Say that you had a wild night tumbling in the hay with a useless cowboy." It was just an offhanded joke. Still she went rigid in his arms. "Tess?"

Her brows dipped. "Useless? No." For longer than was comfortable, she studied him, hard. "I've seen shadows in your eyes, Clancy. Behind that bad boy persona, I see sadness. Why?"

With her still straddling his lap, they were too close for him to avoid her, even turn away. His pulse sped. Trapped. Staring into her eyes made him feel raw and exposed, vulnerable. His chest ached. But what made it difficult to breathe was the knowledge that he had finally dared to take a chance on a woman and push his past aside. After he confessed to the demons inside him, she would walk away. What woman wouldn't?

"Talk to me. Please."

"What is there to say? I come from defective genes."

"Defective genes? I don't understand."

"My father, grandfather and great-grandfather, they were all the same. Mean as hell, drunks and abusers." He shrugged, even as his throat narrowed with emotion. He tried to swallow, but like always it lodged midthroat making it hard to continue. "You see, the acorn doesn't fall far from the tree."

Her eyes grew misty.

Dammit. Clancy recognized sympathy when he saw it, because he'd seen it before in those who knew the truth, but he didn't deserve Tess's compassion, because he hadn't taken the brunt of his father's anger. Sure, his old man had knocked him around from time to time, especially when he attempted to protect his mother, who had been the true object of his father's fury. He wasn't able to save her any more than he could save himself.

"My mother didn't leave on her own accord. She left before my father killed her."

Tess's expression of horror made his stomach clench. Then she did the unexpected. She threw her arms around his neck and hugged him close.

"I'm so sorry, Clancy."

As she continued to murmur comforting words in his ear, he grabbed her wrists, peeling her away from him. "Tess, don't you understand? I'm my father's son."

She slowly eased back, her arms dropping to her side. "What?" As she stared at him, his heart threatened to burst from his chest. "You can't believe that." When he didn't speak, she shook her head. "This is what Jessie was talking about?"

"Jessie?" She couldn't—wouldn't have betrayed him. Not after all they had been through.

"She said that you don't see yourself as a caring, loving man. Clancy, you are that and so much more. Look what you're doing for Milo, for Julie, for me and my family."

"Julie is a child. It was the right thing to do. And I haven't done much for you and your family besides be a decent neighbor. Neighbors help neighbors."

"That's not true," she said adamantly.

God help him, she had to understand. "You don't know anything about me. What would you say if I told you that my sexual taste runs a little rough?"

She licked her lips. "How rough?"

"Remembered the D-links in my bedroom ceiling?" He paused, waiting for a response.

"Y-yes."

"Would you let me blindfold you, bind your wrists, and do whatever I choose?" The image he painted of her in his mind made his softened cock firm. Since he remained partially inside her, her eyes widened at his bodily reaction.

Her chest rose and fell on heightened breaths. "Whatever you choose?"

"Hot and cold play. Ice. Wax. Nipple clamps. Paddles. Whips. Spurs." When he cupped her ass she startled, but didn't show disgust. Slowly he pulled her cheeks apart, before he ran a finger between them to her anus. "I'd take you here." He applied pressure against the puckered skin.

Tess gasped. Her breathing more pronounced.

Shit. If he didn't know better, he'd say she was aroused. When her nipples beaded and she softened into him, he knew he was in trouble.

"Yes," she hissed.

"Don't you know it's dangerous to put yourself in that position with someone you don't know? That's why the ménages. I don't trust myself."

She leaned so close that their lips brushed his. "But I trust you."

Every tendon and muscle in his body tightened. "Dammit, Tess, you shouldn't."

Chapter Sixteen

Naked and straddling Clancy's hips as he described the vileness that had raged through the male population of his family should have scared Tess. Instead trepidation and excitement collided inside her. If she hadn't firsthand witnessed how caring Clancy could be, how tenderly he made love, she would be screaming and running for the hills. But Jessie was right. Clancy was a man worthy of love, if he only believed it.

"So what would you say if I told you that I fantasize of being bound and taken by a strong man, one who knows what he wants? Who takes what he wants." Just the thought of allowing him to dominate her sent her heart racing.

"Damn you, Tess." He sank back against the couch as if he attempted to put distance between them. "You're making this hard."

She glanced down where their bodies came together. "Yes. It is." The musky scent of their lovemaking surrounded them.

The vein running down his forehead protruded. He growled, low and long, before he brutally smashed his mouth over hers. Their teeth clinked, his tongue pushing between her lips to ravish her. If he was trying to frighten her, this was a helluva way, with his cock buried inside her while he kissed her mindlessly.

His large hands smoothed up her back, until one tangled in her hair. He yanked her head back, breaking their caress and exposing her neck to him. She half expected him to give her a hickey. Instead he trailed featherlight kisses down her neck, chest, pulling on her hair to force her back to arch into him.

Gliding a palm over a breast, he teased a nipple with his fingers and then squeezed with enough pressure that she gasped at the pleasure-pain radiating through the globe. Then he replaced his thumb and index finger with his moist mouth, flattening his tongue against the hardened peak and flicking it several times before he began to suck. Her eyes closed in ecstasy, springing open when he pinched the other nipple, hard.

Every pore in her body ignited into flames. Desire pooled between her thighs, her arousal soaring as if it had wings.

"Clancy." His name came out a breathy plea.

"Do you like this, darlin'? Like a little pain with your lovin'?"

She thrust her hips back and forth. The movement rubbed her clit against him as his cock stroked the back of her pussy. A handful of spasms burst in all directions, taking her closer and closer to where she wanted to be.

"Yes. God. Yes." She staggered on the verge of release when bright car lights beamed through the parted living-room curtains. "Crap! They're home." As she sprung from Clancy's lap, she almost fell back. "*Oh. Shit. Shit. Shit.*" His fingers were still wound in her hair. Frantically they worked to untangle themselves. When they were successful, both of them moved at once.

As she snatched up her clothes and shoes, Clancy did the same.

"You take the hall bathroom." She was already running for her bedroom when she heard a car door slam. She stepped into her room, turning to lock the door behind her. Her heart pounded so hard she thought it would leap from the walls of her chest. When the doorknob twisted, rattled, she nearly swallowed her tongue.

"Tess?" Rose's muffled voice bled from beneath the door. "Everything okay?"

"Yeah. Sure. I'm just changing my clothes."

"Why?"

"Because I sat in something at the Peterson's." The lie came easily, but she still hung her head in shame.

"Clancy's truck is outside. Where is he?"

He's naked, hiding in the hall bathroom.

"Hell, I don't know. Try the kitchen or bathroom." She regretted barking at her sister the second the snippy words left her mouth. Taking a breath to steady herself, she added, "Keep him occupied. I'll be out in a minute." Then she tossed her clothes in a corner of the room and hurried toward her closet.

After donning a fresh pair of jeans and a soft, thin, pink sweater, she glanced at the clock and noted that it was only seven thirty. Her siblings must have been worried about her. That alone made her feel horrible. As she exited her bedroom, she heard laughter coming from the living room. Clancy fit in with her family. In fact, he seemed to fit everywhere. Only he couldn't see the truth.

Dressed and wearing his Stetson, Clancy stood when she walked into the room. When he raised his gaze to meet hers, mischief danced in his eyes. She couldn't help grinning. They had almost gotten caught. Not to mention, he was so good looking. She wanted to go to him, put her arms around him, but she didn't.

"Ready?" Levi got to his feet, their sisters following.

"Ready?" Tess repeated.

He shot a questioning look at Clancy and then back at her.

"We're going back to the Peterson's," Clancy clarified. "You're riding with me."

"Oh. Okay."

He stepped forward and placed a palm at the small of her back. His touch spread warmth throughout her. For a moment she marveled at how things had changed so quickly between them. One minute she was cursing him, the next screwing him.

As they walked out of house and headed to his truck, he never stopped touching her. If Levi or her sisters noticed, they didn't show it. The three of them seemed self-absorbed, even excited, laughing and chatting, apparently eager to get back to the barbeque. She watched as they got into her brother's vehicle and pulled away.

When she turned around, Clancy had the passenger side door open. She climbed inside and he shut the door before moving to the other side and sliding behind the wheel.

He started the engine. "You're smiling."

Was she?

Midway through buckling her seatbelt she paused. "It just dawned on me that this is my brother and sisters' first real show of happiness since before the funeral."

He shifted the truck in gear and the truck began to move. "And what about you?"

"I'm beginning to think our move to San Antonio was a good decision."

Growing quiet, he pulled onto the street. "Tess, we should probably discuss this thing between us."

Not tonight. For the next couple of hours she wanted to be carefree and throw caution to the wind. She wanted to dance and sing and if the opportunity arose, make love to the sexy cowboy sitting next to her.

"Fine, but not this evening. Tonight is about fun." She reached over and turned up the radio and Tim McGraw's voice filled the cabin.

"Fun?" A boyish grin spread across Clancy's handsome face. "I can do fun."

He was a man of his words.

The second his truck stopped behind another one in front of the Peterson's, he reached over the console, pulled her into his arms and kissed her. Not a friendly peck, but one that held strength and desire and a promise of something better to come.

A bang against the window tore them apart. Tess jerked her gaze around to come eye to eye with her brother and he didn't look happy. Face beet-red, he scowled.

Narrowing his steely glare toward Clancy, he growled, "Get out, Tess."

Her eyes widened in surprise. Levi had never spoken to her like that and he wouldn't start now. As she moved to open the door, Clancy's fingers closed around her arm, hauling her back against the seat.

"Let me talk to him." He opened his door and stepped out of the vehicle.

Levi nearly flew around the truck.

A cry welled up in her throat, but it was too late. Levi smacked his palms against Clancy's chest and shoved. As Clancy stumbled backward, Tess sucked in a terse breath. Desperately she clawed for the door handle and jerked it open, and nearly fell out in her haste. From somewhere behind she heard her sisters scream. The sound of running feet followed.

"That's my sister." Levi's lips curled into a snarl.

Thank God, Clancy made no attempts to defend himself. He simply narrowed his eyes on her brother.

Fist clenched, Levi stepped forward.

"Levi, *stop* this." But he was too focused on the man before him to listen to her.

In a series of quick twists and turns, movements so quick they left Tess speechless, Clancy embraced Levi from behind, her brother's arms pinned to his side.

He kicked, twisted. Cursed. "Let. Me. Go."

"*Stop it!*" Tess shrieked. "*Stop it. Now!*"

"Best listen." Barely leashed anger in Clancy's soft spoken words held enough of a threat to still Levi and make Tess's skin crawl.

Wide-eyed, Rose and Rachel screeched to a halt beside her.

"Ohmygod," Rose breathed. "What—"

"He kissed her," Levi snapped.

Rose's surprised expression mirrored Rachel's. Silence stretched between the two girls. Then, as if their next move was choreographed, they burst into a choir of laughter.

Levi struggled. All attempts to gain his freedom were futile. "Let me go."

"You'll behave?" Clancy asked.

Levi's jaws clenched together, but in the end he reluctantly nodded.

Clancy released Tess's brother, but took a defensive position and parted his feet and clenched his fists, just in case the foolish boy changed his mind. Rose and Rachel were still hee-hawing. Tess continued to frown, but her eyes shined with concern.

"I'm glad you find this funny," Levi grumbled, wiping his palms down his jeans.

"It was a kiss." Rose chuckled.

"Yeah. And we know where that leads," he countered, squaring his hat on his head.

Tess raised her hands to her waist and lowered her chin so she stared up through feathered lashes at him. "Uhm...maybe you should tell me exactly where a kiss leads."

A blush rose up the boy's neck, sweeping across his cheeks. He tugged on the brim of his hat nervously. "We don't need his help."

"I'll make that determination."

"But, Tess—"

"You need to apologize."

"The hell you say. He kissed you."

"No. I kissed him. There's a big difference."

"What?" her siblings said in unison.

"I like him, and I'll continue to kiss him as long as I want."

Her words and her protective stance sent goose bumps across Clancy's skin. He could fall in love with this woman.

Levi's startled gaze darted from Clancy to his sister. "Tess, you can't be serious."

She leveled a heated stare on him. "As a heart attack. Now I suggest the three of you find something else to do."

Rose and Rachel nodded and turned to leave.

Levi held his ground, not ready to accept her dictate. "Tess, maybe we should take this home and discuss it."

"There's nothing to discuss. *This* concerns Clancy and me. Do I make myself clear?"

Clancy didn't realize until she glanced at him that he was grinning like a damned idiot. It pleased him even further when she walked into his arms, and in front of her family, she planted another kiss on him.

"Fuck," Levi grumbled.

"Watch your language," Tess murmured against Clancy's lips, before she eased back. "Either you can find something to do or you can get your ass back into that truck and go home. Your choice."

"Fine," Levi barked and turned, stomping off.

When they were finally alone, Clancy whispered, "I think that went well."

"You okay?"

"I'm more than okay." He cupped the back of her head and urged her lips closer to his. "You're pretty scary when you're mad."

"Don't forget it." Her brief kiss teased his mouth. "Now how about that fun you promised? I'm in the mood to dance."

"Then dancing it is."

Pride burst from his chest as he led her through the parking area and out upon the makeshift dance floor. Fortunately a slow dance played and he pulled her close. Breathing in her feminine essence, he took a step and she followed, and in seconds she danced away with his heart.

How could a woman feel so perfect cuddled against him, but she did. He buried his face into her sweet-smelling hair. From the corner of his eye he saw Levi glaring at him.

Who could blame the boy for being angry?

His precious sister had just hooked up with the scoundrel of San Antonio. When the opportunity arose, he'd talk to Levi. Let him know his intentions toward Tess were honorable.

Honorable?

He huffed out loud, drawing her attention. As he stared into the depths of her eyes, he wondered if he even knew the meaning of that word. His father certainly hadn't.

"Everything all right?" she asked.

"It would be better if I had you alone."

Just then someone tapped on Clancy's shoulder. He turned to find Clint Junior, Wade's eldest brother, gazing down upon Tess.

The tall, athletically built man tipped his Stetson. "May I?" Quiet sophistication surrounded Clint as he smiled, the gesture not quite making it to his eyes. Since he'd returned from the Marines, he had the demeanor of a man with something burdensome on his mind, not the carefree teen Clancy remembered.

Dammit. He didn't want another man touching her. Yet it wasn't his decision. "Lady's choice," he said begrudgingly.

Clint took her hand and Clancy felt irritation crawl across his skin. *Mine*, whispered emphatically through his head. But she wasn't his—not by a long shot.

When Clint waltzed away with his woman, Clancy backed off the dance floor.

"Looks like the two of you have found some common ground."

He pivoted to find Jessie grinning like a Cheshire cat. "I like her, Jessie."

Her expression softened. "I know."

Uncomfortable with the emotions tugging at his chest, he ripped off his hat and threaded his fingers through his hair. "I've never felt like this."

She reached out and squeezed his arm. "I know."

"So what do I do?"

"Nothing. Just let it happen."

When he saw Becky beating a path toward them, he grabbed Jessie's hand. "Looks like we need to dance."

As they shuffled across the floor, he kept an eye on Tess, making sure that when the song ended he stood next to her.

"Hey, Clint. How 'bout taking your sister-in-law for a spin." Jessie moved into the man's arms before he could answer. "Have fun, you two," she threw over a shoulder as the music began and carried them away.

"Clancy?" Becky's voice crept across his skin, making it tighten uncomfortably. Judging by Tess's hardened expression, she wasn't happy either. "You promised me another dance." She pushed out her bottom lip and waited for an answer.

"You'll have to settle for his wing-man." Ty stepped from the crowd and came to Clancy's rescue. With big, puppyish eyes, he pouted playfully. "Don't break my heart."

Becky chuckled at his antics. Ty had a way with women, from three to ninety-three. The smooth-talker and his teasing nature drew women like bees to honey.

"I wouldn't think of it." She stepped into his embrace.

Ty winked, mouthing, "You owe me."

When they were out of earshot, Clancy took a breath of relief. "He'll have his hands full this evening."

Tess flashed Becky an expression of dislike. "Better him than you."

"My sentiments exactly." He drew her close. "Now, where were we?"

"You were about to ask me if I want to go for a walk." Moonlight shining down upon her face made her appear ethereal.

My angel, whispered through his mind.

"Your wish is my command." Throwing an arm around her shoulder, he walked her off the dance floor. Just before they slipped into the darkness of the night, Levi joined them.

"So are we still on for tomorrow?" He pulled his brows together in a contemplating expression that didn't fool Clancy as the boy continued. "I was thinking about purchasing a Charolais bull or maybe a cow to breed to our Angus or Tommy Keegan's Hereford. I hear Charolais produce more red meat and less fat. There's a "red factor" Charolais cow two counties over for sale. Or we could look for some young calves to experiment on."

Okay. So maybe this wasn't a ploy to keep his sister from disappearing into the night with Clancy. Clearly Levi had done his homework if he realized the breed standards not only accepted the almost pure white cattle, but also the light red ones.

"Wow. You've put a lot of thought into this, haven't you?" The twinkle in Tess's eye revealed she wasn't buying it. "Perhaps we could discuss this tomorrow."

"Sure. Oh, hey, Clancy. What are your thoughts on Charbrays?"

Tess glanced toward Clancy.

"It's an offspring of Charolais crossed with a Brahma," he explained. "It is recognized as a breed in its own right."

"Good to know." She smiled, threading her arm through Clancy's and giving him a tug toward the shadows.

Levi frowned, but must have caught himself, because he cleared his throat. "So would you say Angus, Hereford, or Brahma, are the smarter choice?"

Before Clancy could answer, Tess did. "I think the smart thing to do is to accept this thing between Clancy and me. Good night, Levi."

"But, Tess—"

"Good night, Levi," she repeated.

Discouraged, he shook his head and walked off.

Clancy raised the back of her hand to his lips. "Can't blame him for trying."

She sighed. "This isn't going to be easy."

"Nothing worth having ever is." He leaned down and closed his mouth over hers. "So what do you say we slip into the shadows and let me have my way with you?" he muttered against her lips.

"Hmmm...sounds like it has potential."

He glanced around for Levi before he pulled her deeper into the darkness.

Chapter Seventeen

Waking in a daze, Tess yawned until her bottom jaw ached. She needed coffee, so much so that when she climbed out of bed and couldn't find her slippers, she stepped barefoot out into the hall.

Late nights had become a norm since she and Clancy had revealed their feelings about each other. Only when he left for Austin on business did they spend evenings apart.

Most of the their time together was going to dinner, taking a walk or ride, and long talks or just peaceful silence shared between them on the porch swing. Occasionally they found precious moments to make love, but for all his previous talk of blindfolds and whips, he never introduced them to her. When she brought up the subject, he kissed her in a way that she lost track of time, as well as what they were talking about.

Of course, those times together were limited since Milo and Julie had taken over Clancy's house and Levi watched them like a hawk or insisted on tagging along when they went out. It was becoming more and more difficult to find time alone. She knew at some point she would have to have a heart-to-heart with her brother, but for now it seemed more important that they work to come together as a family.

Half-asleep, she shuffled her way to the kitchen, the rich smell of coffee and bacon leading the way. As usual her siblings were up and preparing for the chores ahead of them. Only she had grabbed an extra hour of sleep on this lazy Saturday. Placing a palm against the door, she heard someone say her name and she stopped short, listening.

"Give her a break, Levi," Rachel grumbled. "Do you have any idea what she's given up for us?"

"Hell yes. But he isn't good enough for her."

"And who assigned you the morality judge," Rose snapped. "You know you're not a perfect angel. I saw you with that Peterson girl."

Now that caught Tess's attention. For a moment, she wondered what hot water Levi had gotten himself into. Then again, maybe ignorance was bliss. She eased closer to the door, her drooping eyelids now wide open.

"She's happier than I've ever seen her. Haven't you seen the way she looks at him?" Rachel's voice softened. "It's like how Mom used to look at Dad."

Chills raced across Tess's arms. Her pulse flickered alive.

Her mother had once told Tess that her heart would know when she found true love, even if her mind fought the truth. The memory of her mother's soft laughter and words stroked the recess of Tess's mind. *"Baby, you probably won't even like him. Lord knows that's how it started between me and your dad."*

Tess collapsed against the cool, stucco wall. Had she fallen in love with Clancy?

In all honesty, Wednesday and Thursday nights had been horrible without him, not seeing him, not kissing him goodnight. Only after he'd called each night and they spent an hour, almost two, talking, could she finally fall asleep.

"She could be happy with someone else. Someone who would treat her right." Tess heard her brother blow out a frustrated breath. "Someone who hasn't been with every damn woman in the State of Texas.

Although Levi's comment hurt, the past was the past. She wouldn't dwell on Clancy's other women any more than she wanted him to brood over the men she'd had in her life. She would rather focus on the fact she planned to be his last.

"You'd have to be blind not to see the way Clancy looks at Tess. Levi, the man's in love with her." Rose nearly growled the revelation.

A smile slid across Tess's face. Was he in love with her? A wave of warmth undulated through her body, almost as if she could feel Clancy's arms close around her. She couldn't wait until this afternoon.

"Yeah, but—"

Tess feigned coughing, silencing Levi before she pushed open the door. "Good morning." She glanced to the half-full coffee pot. "Thank God, coffee."

"You know your butt wouldn't be dragging if you got to bed a little earlier."

Ohmygod. Her eighteen-year-old brother did not just say that to her. He sounded like a mother hen, and it was finally getting irritating.

"Yeah, but she wouldn't be smiling ear to ear if she had." Rose chuckled and Rachel joined in.

Levi's expression hardened. "You know there is a lot to do around here today."

As Tess slipped into a chair and grabbed a piece of crispy bacon off the plate in the center of the table, she leveled her sight on him. "Is there something you're getting at?" She took a bite and chewed. The smoky taste made her stomach grumble with hunger.

Fork in hand, he chased a piece of uneaten egg around his plate. "I'm just saying, hope you don't have any plans for today."

"As a matter of fact I do." She inhaled the steamy coffee before she took a careful sip. Awww...now that's what she needed. "I'm going riding with Clancy."

"But—"

"Back off, Levi." Three sets of startled eyes nailed Rachel. Usually the quiet and least confrontational one of the bunch, she made her stance on the subject known, before she turned to Tess. "One or two eggs?" She pushed to her feet.

"One," Tess replied, still stunned by her sister's outburst. A quick glance in Levi's direction found him looking a little browbeaten. "Come with us this afternoon."

Levi's eyes widened. "Me? Why?"

She couldn't help the grin tugging at her mouth. "Clancy has something he wants to show us."

His brows dipped suspiciously. "What?"

"I don't know, but we'll join him at his place around noon."

Rachel set a plate before Tess. "What about us?"

"Thank you." Tess reached for the salt and pepper to season her egg. "You're welcome to come too."

The legs of Rose's chair scraped across the floor as she stood and began to clear the table. "I think the mall sounds more inviting. How 'bout it, sis?"

Rachel shrugged. "Okay."

"But first we need to muck the stalls," Levi reminded them.

"Agrhhh..." the twins moaned.

As her sisters cleaned up, Tess finished her breakfast. Neither of her siblings tarried, but left promptly to start their chores. It took Tess longer to get motivated, but finally she headed back to her bedroom and donned a pair of old jeans and a long-sleeved shirt, before heading out the door.

The grinding of heavy equipment moaned in the distance, joined by Levi's all-terrain-vehicle. The whine of his four-wheeler stopped when he shut off the engine and strolled toward her.

She should have known Levi would be all over something that was happening adjacent to their property. "What's going on?"

"Looks like the Jensen's must have sold the land that abuts the back of ours. They're clearing the trees along the fence line and look to be digging a stream and pond to catch the runoff from the mountains." He took off his hat and wiped the sweat from his forehead. "Wish we could have purchased that land." The wistfulness in his voice bothered her, but she hadn't had a choice.

"That would have taken all our savings. We couldn't take the chance. Not knowing exactly how this venture would work out."

"I know. I was just saying." He raised a shoulder and let it fall. Then he sighed. "C'mon. There's a pile of horse manure with your name on it."

She slapped him playfully on the back.

For the next four hours she shoveled shit, carried some to the garden where Rose and Rachel pulled weeds, then it was back to the barn to clean out the tack room. By the time eleven o'clock rolled around, her shoulders, back and arms hurt. She was ready to call it quits. Pulling off her gloves, she placed them in the bin inside the barn and strolled into the bright sunlight and the rather hot day. Her only savior was a cool breeze that wafted by. She took a moment to breathe in the fresh scent of pine with a hint of her own perspiration and manure.

This land was truly beautiful.

When a set of strong arms slid around her, she smiled up at Levi.

He squeezed. "Day dreamin', sis?"

She laughed, amazed at how easily the musical sound came from her these days. "It's beautiful here."

He held her for a moment while a mockingbird perched on their roof sang the prettiest song she had ever heard. Twitching its long tail, the bird spread its gray wings with white patches and pushed off, flying away.

"You really like him, don't you?"

"Yes. I do." She turned in his embrace, wrapping her arms around his waist. "He makes me happy."

"I can see that." He pressed his cheek to her forehead. "I'm just worried."

"I know you are, but I'm a big girl. I'll make mistakes, but I'm hoping Clancy isn't one of them. And if you're worried about the ranch—"

"God, Tess, that's not it at all. I don't want to see you hurt. You deserve— I mean, I want—" When it appeared his emotions became too much, he quit trying to explain and released her. "We'd best be getting ready."

Clancy swung the saddle up on the last horse's back just as Levi's truck pulled into his driveway. The second he saw Tess get out, his heart began to pound like a randy schoolboy's. The urge to go to her, to take her in his arms, almost won over securing the cinch around the large bay gelding.

When they joined him at the hitching post outside the barn, he found it difficult not to reach for her. Fortunately, he didn't have to refrain from touching her as she walked up to him, tilting her chin to receive his welcoming kiss. Slipping his arms around her, he noted how good she felt and smelled. Amongst her soft perfume was the fresh scent of soap and shampoo. Reluctant to let her go when their short caress ended, he left an arm around her, half expecting to see Levi glaring at him, but he was wrong.

With a sheepish expression, the boy moved toward Clancy and extended him his hand. "Wiseman."

Shocked but pleased, Clancy released Tess and stepped forward, clasping hands. "Levi."

Did this mean the tension between them had come to an end? God. He hoped so. Tess's happiness meant everything to him. She wouldn't be content with controversy within her family. When she gifted them both with a bright smile Clancy knew things were heading in the right direction.

"So where are we going?" Levi ran his fingertips down the bay's forehead to his soft muzzle. The act of kindness appeared so natural. Clancy had no doubts the boy was meant for ranching. He had a love of the land and all things on it.

"I thought we would ride the fence line. Then take a break and have a picnic. Hope you like roast beef sandwiches and potato salad."

Confusion tugged at Levi's brows and Tess mirrored her brother's expression. "Uhhh...sure. Roast beef is fine."

Clancy could see in her eyes she had expected something more than a ride and picnic. Anxiety skittered across his arms. "Saddle up." Hopefully his surprise wouldn't blow up in his face.

Bella, his dapple mare, clawed the ground, ready to stretch her long legs, but Tess had captured his attention. Without a second thought, she slipped a booted-foot into the stirrup of a Palomino he'd chosen just for her as she grabbed the saddle horn, and hoisted herself atop the saddle.

Damn. She looked good sitting on a horse. Just the type of woman he could see himself settling down with. Strong. Independent. And intelligent. Yet all woman, and he knew every curve, valley and mound on that beautiful body.

"Hey, Wiseman. We gonna ride or stand here and stare at my sister?"

This time the boy offered him a cocky smile, while Tess giggled softly and dug her heels into the sides of the Palomino. Without pause, Clancy mounted his horse and kicked her sides. Bella lurched forward in an effort to catch up with the others.

As they rode through acre after acre of rocky hills and meadows, the sun beamed down upon them. It was warmer than he had expected and he gave thanks for the occasional breeze that whispered through the tree branches, but due to the work being done in the distance, the wind carried the scent of freshly churned dirt. He had wanted this day to be perfect. So when he heard the machinery pause and stop to rising voices, trepidation slid across his skin. Something must have gone wrong.

"Must have struck caliche," Levi offered.

Clancy calmed a little. The boy was probably right, because Clancy had had more encounters with the hard, clay subsoil then he cared to remember. Damn stuff always seemed to be where he wanted to dig. Reining his horse toward the now growing chaos, he didn't wait for Tess, and Levi followed.

When the foreman on the job saw them, Clancy swung off his mare and hastened on foot to join him. As Richard Flayer approached, he jerked off his hat and ran the back of his gloved hand over his damp forehead. "You're not going to believe this." The man's face was flushed. His hands trembled.

Clancy didn't like the sound of this. "What's wrong?"

"Well, boss." He hesitated, taking a steadying breath. "We dug up a body."

"A what?" Surely he hadn't heard the man correctly. He carefully eased between the tight strands of barbed-wire fencing.

"A body. I had the men stop immediately. The sheriff has been called." As Clancy climbed off his horse, Richard continued. "We didn't want to disturb anything, in case...

Well... Hell, Mr. Wiseman, I've never dealt with anything like this."

And neither had Clancy.

It barely registered that Tess and Levi were hot on their heels as they crossed the uneven terrain toward where a large bulldozer and a loader sat silently. A crowd of workmen had gathered around a fallen tree. Clancy edged his way through the line of men and came to an abrupt stop. The bony skeleton remains of a hand jutted through the softened earth.

Levi's wide-eyed gaze darted toward Tess and then Clancy. "Is that a hand?"

"Levi, why don't you take your sister and the horses back to the barn. Have Milo unsaddle them and put them away. I'll catch a ride with Richard."

Tess sidled up to him. "We'll take care of it." She leaned closer, whispering, "I take it this wasn't what you wanted to show us."

"No, darlin'." He circled his arms around her waist and pulled her to him. She felt so warm, so soft against him. "The deed for this land came through yesterday. I thought maybe we could run Wiseman and Gilmore cattle on it. After they finished the stream and pond, cleared the ground in this vicinity, I instructed them to put a couple of gates between the properties."

"Really?" Levi's voice rose with new life. "Hot damn!" Just as soon as the words burst from his mouth his face colored with embarrassment. He slid his gaze toward the remains, choking down his excitement. "Sorry."

As Clancy held Tess, in a show of support he reached out with one hand, grasped the boy's shoulder, squeezed and released. Whatever happened here was horrible, but he doubted whoever lay beneath the earth would begrudge Levi a little happiness.

"You'll call us when you know something?" Tess asked.

"Of course." His mouth brushed hers, and then he let her go.

He watched them mount and ride off. Before they disappeared from sight, Tess turned and waved. He raised his hand in return only allowing it to drift to his side when they were gone, and then he faced the remains once again.

He hadn't realized how much this discovery had affected his foreman, until he spoke again. "What do you think happened?" Weariness hung in Richard's tone.

"Beats me."

Clancy had known the Jensens forever.

It was incomprehensible that they had been involved with what appeared to be foul play. When he was a child he'd hung out with several of their grandchildren who came to visit during the summer. Joined them occasionally for dinner. Lloyd and Camilla had always appeared to be loving grandparents, but Clancy knew firsthand how deceiving appearances could be.

"Boss, want us to move to the fence line and start tearing it down?"

"Better wait for the police."

Shortly after Sheriff Paul McGrath arrived and introductions were made, Richard told his story once more. After which the sheriff hastened to clear the immediate area, which included Clancy's crew, with the exception of those directly involved in the discovery. Some lollygaggers remained and watched from a designated distance as forensic personnel taped and charted off the area. Other individuals skedaddled as if the devil himself were after them, or maybe they were simply happy to have the weekend off or, more likely, spread the gossip.

Picture after picture documented the location before they began to unearth the body. From Clancy's vantage point he thought he recognized pieces of tattered material that appeared to be denim, but jeans in this country were the norm. In the meantime, the sheriff and another policeman began to interrogate those left behind.

As the sun shifted in the sky, Clancy thought he saw something gleam amongst the loose dirt. A male technician must have seen the same thing, because he took what looked like a paintbrush and swept the dirt aside. With his camera he took a snapshot before he bagged and labeled whatever he found.

Clancy's stomach growled, reminding him that he hadn't eaten anything since early that morning. The lunch he packed was probably growing stale in his saddlebags. The thought emerged just as twigs and rocks popping beneath tires of an approaching vehicle forced him to look over his shoulder. He smiled and turned around. Tess parked her car behind Richard's work truck. When she got out, she held a picnic basket looped around her arm.

Since the area was secure and he doubted the narrow-eyed officer would let her pass, he went to her. By the time he reached her, she had a tablecloth spread across the hood of her car, iced tea, assorted fruits and sandwiches atop of it.

"Thought you might be hungry."

He gathered her into his arms. "A woman after my own heart." Then he savored her lips, before whispering, "Sorry about today."

"No worries." She brushed a lock of hair out of his eyes. "Maybe tonight you can make up for it." Desire flickered in her eyes and his groin tightened.

"Hmmm...do we have to wait until tonight?" He smoothed his palms up and down her bare arms. "Milo and Julie found a place yesterday. They moved out this morning. How 'bout dinner at my place?" He rubbed his nose against hers, thinking of how nice it would be to have her all alone with no one to interrupt them. "And maybe you'd consider breakfast too."

"Breakfast?" She made a soft sound in his ear just as his stomach growled. Easing back from his embrace, she smiled. "Perhaps you should first start with lunch. Eat."

While he ate, she quizzed him about what had happened so far. He had little to say, because as of yet he still hadn't spoken to the sheriff. Just as he took the final bite of his tuna sandwich, McGrath walked up.

He tipped his hat. "Ma'am."

She smiled prettily and the damn man slid an interested gaze over her. Clancy threw an arm around her shoulders, pulling her close.

"So that's your land just past the fence line? And you just recently relocated from California?" the sheriff repeated.

"Yes." Tess slipped from beneath Clancy's arm and began to put everything back into the picnic basket.

"Hmmm..." His steely gaze pinned Clancy. "Wiseman, any idea who this is?"

What the hell? Clancy furrowed his brows. "Not even a hint. Why?"

"Because the skull of our victim is pretty damaged, as if she took quite a wallop to the head. We found these." The sheriff unfurled his fingers to display two plastic evidence bags. One contained a set of wedding rings, the other a locket. "Ever seen 'em before?"

Clancy's heart stopped. He couldn't believe his eyes. Eyes that blurred, going black around the edges. His lips tightened to a bloodless line of fury and a strangled cry crawled up his throat.

"They're my mother's."

Chapter Eighteen

Tess had heard the phrase *turning white as a sheet*, but she had never seen it before today. Every ounce of blood drained from Clancy's face, returning with a vengeance that chilled her. His neck and face flashed beet-red. He clenched his jaws so tightly that she actually heard his teeth grind. She could have sworn that the tendons in his neck grew so taut they looked as if they would snap. But even his sudden fury didn't compare to the haunted cry that rose as if it had been ripped from his very soul.

"They're my mother's."

Tess froze where she stood. *His mother's?* Hadn't he said his mother left town?

She felt the tremor that raced through him before he snatched his arm from around her shoulders. As if he moved on autopilot, he stepped forward and took the jewelry from the sheriff's outstretched hands. For a moment, he didn't speak, only stared at the dirt-encrusted items bagged and laying in his opened palms.

"Damn him," he growled. His fingers slowly curled into fists, clutching the jewelry. "Damn him to hell."

"Who?" the sheriff asked.

Apparently Clancy didn't hear him, because he didn't answer. Instead his entire body began to shake uncontrollably. Tess wanted to go to him, console him. But no one dared to approach him, not her nor the sheriff who paused, watching him intently.

"Wiseman, are you sure these belong to your mother?"

The sheriff's question seemed to pull Clancy from the dark place that held him in its grip. He jerked his head up as moisture filled his eyes. A single tear slid down his cheek, nearly breaking Tess's heart. While she sucked in a taut breath, he swallowed and inhaled a shaky one, before his features took on a stiff, unapproachable expression.

With eerie detachment, he dropped the jewelry back into the sheriff's hands. "They're hers." Then, without another word, he pivoted and walked away.

"Wiseman, we need to talk." The sheriff's statement didn't slow him.

For a moment Tess couldn't move. When she finally found her legs, she pushed past the police tape and ran after Clancy, catching up with him as he squeezed between the barbed-wire strings. "Wait. I'll go with you."

His backbone went rigid. Slowly he faced her. The coolness in his glare brought her up short. "Go home, Tess."

"Clancy. Please. I want to be there for you—"

"Go. Home."

The measure of indifference in his tone stole her breath. She didn't attempt to follow after that, because suddenly it felt as if something more than the razor-sharp fence lay between them.

"Miss Gilmore." She drifted around to find the sheriff standing behind her, his thick thumbs tucked in his belt. "How well do you know Wiseman and his family?"

Frowning, she stared in disbelief at the burly man with a ketchup stain on his tie. He couldn't possibly be insinuating Clancy had anything to do with this. Even a blind man could have seen the impact it had on Clancy after he realized that his mother had never left San Antonio but had been murdered. It was normal for him to be stunned and hurt, then furious, moving quickly into a cold, emotionless state, shutting down to protect himself.

She knew all about coping skills.

Tess wet her now parched lips. "For just over a month. But I can tell you that he was only fourteen when his mother left town."

But she didn't leave town, not like Clancy believed. That's when everything fell into place.

Tess gasped, covering her mouth with a palm. "His father."

"His father?"

Oh my God. Her hand fell to her side.

"Clancy said his mother left before his father—" Her mouth closed on its own accord, almost as if subconsciously she couldn't bring herself to say the words. She tried to wrap her mind around the idea, but it left her feeling sick to her stomach.

The sheriff cocked a brow, waiting.

"Could kill her." Lord this couldn't be happening. "The man died in an accident the day after..." Her voice drifted off again as they continued to walk toward her vehicle.

Or had Clancy's father deliberately killed himself?

A tremor slithered up her spine. "I don't know anything else. Perhaps you should confirm the woman's identity before questioning Clancy."

The sheriff's eyes widened at her defensive stance.

"I'm sorry, but as you can see, this has obviously been a shock to him. I've never seen him like this."

"Will you be joining him now?"

"No." And she understood him wanting his space at a moment like this.

McGrath reached into a pocket, pulled out a card and handed it to her. "If you think of anything, call me."

She tucked the card in her pocket, and then grabbed the picnic basket off the hood and opened the car door to climb in. Her hand shook as she reached for the key and flipped it over, starting the engine. It took a moment longer to gather her wits. When she did she shifted into reverse, making her way back to her house.

As she drove past Clancy's place, she slowed the car. He didn't want to see her. Like anyone who had lost someone they loved, he probably needed some space—time to mourn—time to adjust to the numbing disbelief and refusal. But it had been the unbearable pain in his eyes so suddenly masked that frightened her. If he attempted to conceal his anguish, he would never heal. Even worse, it could crush him, pulling him deep into a depression like the one that nearly destroyed Rachel after their parents' death.

Tess wasn't aware of her tears until she choked on a sob. Still crying when she pulled into her driveway, she cut the engine and got out. Clancy hurt and there was nothing she could do to help him, except to be there when he was ready to talk.

"Tess?" Glancing up, she meet Levi's concerned gaze. As he grew nearer, his frown deepened. "What is it?"

She swiped at her eyes. "They think it's Clancy's mother."

"But I thought—"

"I know. Until identification is made we won't know, but Clancy is sure the jewelry found is hers."

"Holy crap. Is he okay?"

She shook her head, and then started for the door.

"Is there anything I can do? Maybe help with the stock?"

"That's very kind, Levi. I think what he needs now is some space."

"Yeah. Of course." When he opened the door and stepped aside to allow her entrance, he released the air in his lungs. "That's pretty screwed up, sis."

Weariness seeped into her bones and she collapsed upon the couch. "I can't imagine what he's going through. To think his father killed her."

"What?"

Tess closed her eyes. That was one detail her brother hadn't been privy to, until now. "Levi, you can't say anything. Please keep this just between us because it isn't ours to tell, but Clancy told me that his father was abusive. That's the reason his mother left."

He plopped down on the sofa beside her. "You mean he used to beat her up?" Her brother's innocence was endearing.

Their father had never raised his voice, much less his hand to their mother. He'd cherished her, loved her more than life itself. So it didn't surprise her that Levi found it inconceivable that a man would violently strike a woman, especially someone he was supposed to care about.

"Yes, but I don't think the fact is well-known."

"So what happens now?" he asked.

"My guess is there will be an autopsy to determine cause of death. But being buried out in the middle of someone else's property is pretty telling. Since she's from this area, they can probably use hospital and dental records to identify her. Then there is the jewelry that might be able to be identified through pictures." Now that she recalled, she didn't remember seeing any pictures of Clancy's mother or father in the house.

When the door swung open, slamming against the wall, Rose and Rachel both pushed through it at once. Their eyes were as big as saucers.

Rachel tripped over her feet, nearly falling, while Rose beat a path straight to them. "There's a police car at Clancy's." She took one look at Tess's swollen, red face and paused before asking, "What's going on?"

Rachel sidled up to her twin. "Tess?"

"A body was uncovered on the Jensen property."

Both girls drifted slowly into the same chair, half sitting on each other in the process, except this time there was no pushing and shoving. Instead they silently made room for the other, hanging on every word as Tess explained the situation.

Rachel eyes were moist when she finished. "We have to do something. Bake something."

Rose pushed to her feet. "We should go over there."

"No, Rose. He has enough to deal with. I think Rachel made a lovely suggestion. Why don't the two of you bake something for Clancy? I think he'd like that."

"Then can we take it to him?" Rose asked.

"I'll take it over."

"But, Tess—"

"Give it a rest, Rose." Levi narrowed his sight on her. "Tess will handle it." He got to his feet. "I better finish feeding and locking up the barn." He bent down and lightly kissed Tess on the forehead. "If you need me, I'll be outside."

"Thank you. I think I'll take a shower." Try to wash away the overwhelming helplessness that gripped her like a sharp pair of talons. And maybe when she got out, she'd give Clancy a call.

Sheriff McGrath stared at him across the kitchen table. "So you're saying that your mother was in and out of hospitals due to your father's abuse?"

Clancy felt whipped. How many times would he have to answer the same questions?

"You'll find all her medical records and X-rays at Southwest General. That I remember, she had a broken jaw and collarbone when I was around twelve. He broke her right wrist and one of the bones in the same arm days before she left." Dammit. He had to stop thinking that way. She hadn't left.

Mixed emotions assailed him, making him lightheaded. He tightened his grip on the glass in his hand. Guilt shuddered through him. All these years he had hated her for leaving him with that bastard, only to discover she hadn't.

He threw back a shot of whiskey, relishing the burn before he slammed the tumbler on the table and reached for the bottle. As he poured, he continued.

"We always used Dr. Tadwell as our dentist. You should find evidence of an upper bridge, since the sonofabitch knocked several of her teeth out." That was one night Clancy would never forget. There had been so much blood. "I tried to help, but—" He had been helpless against his father's anger and strength.

As his mother lay broken on the floor, his father had taken Clancy to an urgent care unit. Baseball to the face was the lie. When they returned home, his mother was gone. She had been missing for three days before his father discovered she had taken refuge in a battered woman's shelter. He had been furious. They both had paid when she returned home.

The sheriff scanned the kitchen. "I noticed when I walked through the house that there are no pictures of your parents. Do you have any photographs?"

"They're in the attic."

McGrath made a tsking noise.

Clancy raised his sight to meet McGrath's. "If you're asking whether I killed her? No." He picked up his glass and chugged the contents.

"Maybe you should slow down, Wiseman."

"And maybe you should get the hell out of my house. I've told you all I know. Nothing I say will change things." The burst of laughter that spilled from his mouth sounded scary even to him. "They're both gone. You can't even punish him for what he's done." He poured another drink.

McGrath stared at him across the table. "You don't remember me, do you?"

He raised the tumbler to his lips. "Should I?" He took a swig and swallowed.

"I responded to a call at this location by an anonymous caller twelve years ago. When I arrived, your mother was alone. Evidence pointed to abuse, but she refused to tell me what happened."

Clancy had made that call while his father had filled out the required paperwork at the urgent care facility. Judging by the keen look in the sheriff's eyes, he knew it.

"I suggested that she get in touch with someone—get some help."

Again sarcasm pushed between Clancy's lips in the form of laughter. "And she did just that, but he ended up finding her."

"I'm afraid that's my fault too."

Seeing red, he clenched his jaws.

"I was wet behind the ears, didn't know that ol' Sheriff Davis was your father's friend and drinking buddy until it was too late. When he read my report, he questioned me about the two shelters I recommended." McGrath ran his hand over his head. "Davis was as crooked as a second-hand nail. I never heard anything more about your mother's case. Probably because the sheriff insisted that all calls go through him."

"You're fuckin' kidding me?" This time he tipped the bottle to his lips and took a long pull from it. When he set the bottle down, he shook his head.

"We run things a little differently now that Davis is dead and I'm in charge. I know this doesn't help, but I'm sorry."

The doorbell rang, but Clancy ignored it, choosing to stare at his half-empty bottle of whiskey. "He didn't even have the balls to bury her on our own land." No coffin. No headstone. Just a large oak tree to mark the spot where his mother lay.

When the bell chimed again, the sheriff got up from his chair. "I'll get it on my way out."

"No need. Just tell whoever it is to go away."

McGrath stopped in the doorway. "Those pictures?"

"Yeah. I'll get them to you tomorrow." But tonight he planned to get shitfaced. He poured himself another drink.

"Clancy?"

When he heard Tess's sweet voice, every muscle and tendon in his body tensed. Studying the amber liquid in his tumbler, he didn't bother looking up. Maybe she would get the hint. Instead her boots clicked across the kitchen floor.

"Go away, Tess."

"You don't mean that."

Slowly he raised his head and glared her way. Several food storage containers filled her arms. The scent of garlic touched his nose, but the smell only served to churn his stomach.

Why the hell did people think food helped during times like these? Any cowboy worth his weight knew only whiskey eased the pain. He picked up his glass and tossed the alcohol down.

"Clancy, maybe you should eat something."

He harrumphed. "I haven't had a mother for over twelve years. I don't need one now."

Ignoring him, she moved farther into the room, placed the containers on the table, and went to the cabinet to retrieve a plate. He heard one of the drawers open and silverware clink.

When she set everything down, she took a seat across from him.

"What do you want, Tess?"

"I want to help you."

"Why? You've seen with your own eyes what becomes of the women who set out to *help* a Wiseman."

She reached across the table and laid her hand over his. "That's not you, Clancy."

"Really?" He twisted his hand to grab her wrist.

Her eyes widened, but she didn't speak.

He stood up, dragged her around the table until she slammed against his body. "Do you want to see the real me?"

"I see the real you."

"You foolish woman. You see what I allow you to see."

"Then show me, Clancy. Show me who you really are." A dare hung in her shaky words.

He lowered his mouth and kissed her hard, forcing her lips apart with his tongue. She whimpered, her body dissolving into his. Taking what he wanted, he sucked and nipped, loving her cries. When her hands slid up his shirt, her warm palms stroking skin, he softened his caress, losing himself in her. Only when she reached for his belt and tugged, did he realize this wasn't going exactly how he had planned it. Releasing her, he stepped away.

Her chest rose and fell in rapid succession. The pupils of her eyes widened, almost overtaking the soft blue irises. "If you're trying to scare me, you'll have to do better than that."

"Damn you, Tess." He ran his fingers through his mussed hair. "Why can't you just walk away?"

"Because you're worth fighting for."

"Damn you." Unable to help himself, he dragged her back into his embrace and ravished her once more.

When her hand slipped beyond the waistband of his jeans, a tremor raced up his spine. Like a manacle, her fingers closed around his dick and she squeezed. The exquisite pressure made his breath catch. As she slid her hand up and down, he fumbled with the buttons of her shirt. But the damn things never slipped through their holes. Frustrated and beyond aroused, he pulled at each ends of her blouse. Material ripped and buttons flew in every direction. He didn't even try to unfasten the clasps of her bra. Instead he pushed the silk upward to bare her delicious breasts, and watched them rise and fall with each shuddering breath.

Clancy slid one hand down to cup her ass and pull her to him. She hissed as he leaned into her breasts and felt her nipples beading against him. Lifting her slightly, he nudged his cock between her thighs. And damned if she didn't press her hips into him, rubbing and undulating over his now raging erection.

She was testing him, teasing and pushing him to the brink of his limits. Before he did something he'd regret, he plunged his tongue back into her mouth, darting back and forth. If he couldn't have her, he would damn well mimic what he wanted to do to her.

"Clancy," she whispered. "Fuck me. Take me the way you want. Show me everything you think I should be afraid of."

He eased back and looked steadily at her. Tess had no idea what she asked of him. What kind of man he really was.

"Please, Clancy."

Maybe it was the only way. Give her a taste of his deviant appetite.

"Strip. Lay with your chest on the table, your legs spread apart. And Tess—"

Her large doe-eyes stared back at him. "Yes."

"Don't move."

Chapter Nineteen

By the time she heard Clancy re-enter the kitchen, she lay facedown on the table, with her feet on the floor, her legs spread shoulder-width as he had directed. He shuffled his feet behind her. She heard him set several things down with a clunk and her pulse leaped to life. Not being able to see him, not knowing what he was up to, was disconcerting, but no matter what he said, he wouldn't hurt her. She knew he wouldn't. Still, tiny footsteps of anxiety danced across her chilled skin. The awkward position made her feel vulnerable and exposed and yes, aroused. Circulating air teased her wet pussy, while her nipples rubbed against the cold wood surface.

When he nipped an ass cheek, she gasped and jumped. But a palm against her back pushed her back down. "Don't move." Then with his tongue, his teeth and his lips, he nibbled, licked and sucked.

It felt so good, she pressed up into his touch with a soft sigh of pleasure and widened her thighs, needing him to take the party down south, but he never did. Instead, he stepped away. When he returned, something snapped through the air and came down on the table with a thump.

Tess cried out in surprise. Turning her head, she saw a riding crop in his hands with a dozen or so cowhide leather strips on the end.

"Do you know what this is?"

"A whip."

"It's an Egyptian flogger." He dragged the soft straps down her spine and goose bumps rose across her skin. The tickle made her squirm.

"If you move you'll be punished." He retraced the path, but this time the soft hide fell along her side. And, of course, she writhed from the titillation. "You've earned your first punishment."

Punishment? Holy shit!

Tess silently prayed she knew what she had gotten herself into.

What was once gentle and sensual cracked down hard on the top of her thigh, leaving a sting that left her gasping and clawing for the edges of the table. Clancy laved the fiery area with his tongue, slowly easing the pain. As he kissed her skin, his callused hands turned to silk and stroked her body. His touch was just what she needed.

"My mark on your skin is so purttty." His warm breath brushed her ass as he slurred his last word. Whiskey had taken hold of him, which slightly upped her trepidation.

Would he be able to stop if things got out of control? She trembled, but then calmed. She believed in him.

"Are you frightened, Tess?"

"No." He wouldn't scare her away. But when she heard the sharp tear of paper, goose bumps rose. *It's only the package of a condom*, she reassured herself.

"Pick a safe word, a word that tells me you can't take any more."

"I don't need a safe word. I trust you."

He eased the long flails along her moist sex to create an entirely different sensation that made her pussy contract. "Choose a word, Tess." When the crop slid between her folds, moving along so that the leather caressed her clit, she raised her hips to meet it.

"You moved. Now choose a word," he growled.

"Trust," she breathed in anticipation. "Trust means everything."

"Fuck." Mumbling something unintelligible beneath his breath, he snarled, "Don't speak. D-don't say another damn word unless I grant you permission." It wasn't hard to hear the frustration in his voice.

This time she was prepared for the lash that bit into her ass, but she wasn't for the other five that followed. By the time he finished, tears dampened her eyes from the pain, but more so from the sweet, sweet way her body felt. Every nerve ending tingled, her senses heightened to the point she swore she knew exactly where he was in the room even if she couldn't see him. Not to mention, she could smell whiskey, cologne, perfume and her own desire fill the room. And then there was the weeping between her thighs. She couldn't remember ever being this wet or feeling this alive.

Gliding a finger along her swollen slit, he cursed as she moaned and closed her eyes. When something clinked across the table, she raised her eyelids to see four sets of leather and metal manacles. An itch of anxiety skittered across her flesh. He didn't speak, but the scowl on his face spoke loudly. He was bound and determined to frighten her.

Circling her wrist with one of the handcuffs, he fastened it high to the back of a chair and clicked it shut before he reached for her other hand. After he had her bound, he eyed her as if looking for a reaction she didn't give him the pleasure of receiving. Tess knew that if she wanted to get loose, all she had to do was jerk and the chairs would fall over. Plus, her blood simmered with the need to know just where this scenario would lead.

Then he shifted her legs farther apart and shackled her ankles to the table legs. Her heart started to pound and her lips went dry. Her tongue flicked out to moisten them.

"You're beautiful bound. Helpless." Something eerie rose in the way he said that last word.

For the first time since they started this mind game, Tess felt defenseless. Yet instead of fear, a rush of excitement flooded her as she realized she really would be at his mercy. Prove that she trusted him with her body and her love, because she had fallen for him. She wanted to be with this man. Not just an hour here and there, but wake up each morning in his arms. Never had she imagined it was possible to want a man as much as she did at this moment.

"You're mine to do whatever I want with." It wasn't a question but a statement.

Yes. God. Yes.

Then his palm caressed her calf to her knee and smoothed up the inside of her thigh. Light fingertips swept across her heated center and her body came alive. As her pussy spasmed, the need to close her legs became so overpowering, she whimpered, moving her lower half in an attempt to find a way to ease the pulsing ache between her thighs.

"Fuck," he growled. "You make me want to lose myself in you."

Pressing his hips to her ass, he rocked against her, sliding his cock over her wet sex. One more thrust and he pushed into her body, filling her completely, and then he began to move.

In and out, he stroked her arousal higher and higher, while evidently building his as well. His breaths came faster now, and she could hear his ragged swallow as he fucked her nice and slow.

His fingers dug into the curve of her waist as his thighs trembled against hers. "Dammit. This isn't supposed to happen."

No. No. No. She fought her restraints, needing to be eye to eye with him. Make him understand that she wouldn't let him do this to them.

Arching her back, she grinded her ass into him. "What?" she snapped. "That I might like being bound, whipped and fucked? That you're not the monster you've built in your mind?" She jerked harder against her restraints. This was a helluva position to be in when she wanted to rail at him like a mad woman and maybe even shake some sense into him. If only she could face him, touch him. Her high-pitched outburst began to soften. "That maybe you're just a man like any other who prefers a little kink with his sex. Clancy, you're not your father. Now finish this. I need to hold you—kiss you."

Her words must have triggered something inside him because he made a strangled sound and slammed against her, hard and fast—over and over. He panted and snarled, releasing throaty, desperate sounds more animal than human. Time after time, he stroked a spot so deep within she wanted to scream with pleasure. Rocking into him, she was almost where she needed to be when he withdrew, pushed a finger inside her, and then wedged her ass cheeks apart, spreading her own juices over her anus. As a digit disappeared within, her yip of surprise turned into a long groan. She stiffened, breath eluding her. The ring of muscle burned enough to water her eyes, but made her pussy pulse and get impossibly wetter.

"God. What have I done? I'm sorry. I've never done that without proper preparation."

When he started to remove his finger, she cried, "Don't. Please, Clancy. I want to feel you inside me."

"Tess, we shouldn't be doing this. I've had too much to drink. And with you I lose control."

How could she explain to him that, yes, there was pain, but there was so much more. And she loved the fact that he lost control. She gulped down a breath and started to find the right words, when he stepped away, leaving her feeling empty and speechless.

Kneeling, Clancy unfastened one ankle and then the other. "Tonight I stopped." As he stood, *what if he hadn't,* raced through his tortured mind. Thick emotion clawed so fast up his throat it threatened to choke him. "But what about tomorrow or the night after that? What happens if you anger me and I'm drunk?"

He moved to the head of the table, stopped and unsnapped the manacle around her wrist. God, help him. His heart stuttered. He blinked hard, not wanting to believe the red, angry skin that circled her wrist. The same was true with her other one as he revealed it. Guilt and shame nearly bowled him over. But he managed to keep his footing as he rounded the table and assisted her to a sitting position.

Sliding his palms down her bare arms, he massaged one wrist and then the other. Every time he switched hands he raised it to his lips and kissed the blemished flesh. When she pulled away from him, he flinched, easing a little as she threaded her fingers through his hair.

Guiding his gaze to hers, she spoke softly. "Why can't you see the man that I do?"

He swallowed, but the knot in his throat remained. "Because you're only seeing what you want to. There's something dark in me."

She frowned.

Then in an unexpected move, she placed her palms on his chest and shoved, hard. "You know what, Clancy Wiseman? You're full of shit."

What the hell?

When she jumped off the table, landing on her feet, she scowled at him and gave him another push that sent him stumbling. Before he righted himself, she leaned into him and got right into his face. "Where's this big scary man you keep hidden?"

She poked a finger into his chest, and damned if it didn't hurt. But he didn't make any attempts to stop her.

"Show me this deviant monster I'm supposed to be frightened of?"

Whoa... Where had all this fury come from?

Clancy couldn't believe what he was seeing, much less the nasty things she was saying. Tess Gilmore, mild-mannered schoolteacher, stood before him like a rattler coiled, preparing to strike. And he was her target.

"Tess, please."

"Please?" Her breathy laughter held irony as she perched on her toes to get even closer. They were almost nose to nose when she growled, "What? You've probably had four or five shots of whiskey before I arrived? Feeling a little tipsy. Maybe you're even shitfaced." She snarled, showing perfect white teeth, and then once again gave him a shove.

Dammit. He wished she'd stop that.

"Bet you want to hit me," she tossed her head from side to side, "slap me around a little."

"Lord no, Tess." What he wanted was to reach for her, hold her and kiss away the anger furrowing her forehead and thinning her mouth. "I would never strike you." Just the thought of striking her made him sick to his stomach.

Cynicism spread across her face. The look of distrust felt like a knife to his heart. Then she slid her tongue between her lips. "You mean that in this emotionally charged moment, you never thought of hitting me, not once?"

"Absolutely not." He released the air trapped in his lungs. "I would never hurt you."

She rocked back on her heels. When she raised her hands, he prepared himself to be shoved again or possibly even slapped. Instead she cupped his face in her warm palms.

Her taut expression softened. "Of course you wouldn't. Because, Clancy, you don't have it in you to hit a woman or a child. It isn't who you are. Can't you see you're not your father?" Moisture filled her eyes, her chin started to tremble. "You're so much more."

When the first tear fell, he hauled her into his arms. "Shhh, darlin'. Don't cry." Burying her face against his shoulder, he felt the dampness of her distress on his skin. "Baby, please."

Then he just held her. Stroked her hair and body, while he mentally wrestled with the last several minutes. Tess had intentionally angered him in an attempt to force him to see the truth. A primal voice inside his head whispered *you're not like him.* He released a pent-up breath. Even three sheets to the wind, it hadn't crossed his muddled mind to lay a hand on her. Hell. He hadn't even tried to defend himself against her. All he wanted was to take care of her, ease her anger.

A shiver slipped through her and he felt the quiver. "You're cold." He briskly rubbed his hands up and down her arms, separating them. "You should get dressed."

Nose and eyes red and swollen, she tipped her chin up. "I don't want to get dressed. I want you to warm me." She leaned into him, their bodies touching. "Take me to your bed, Clancy."

His pulse leaped. Without overthinking his next move, he scooped her into his arms and made a beeline for his bedroom. Laying her gently on top of his comforter, he worked it down and she scooted upon the sheets. He climbed in beside her and pulled the bedding to their waist, then leaned over and nudged her nose with his, before he lightly pressed his lips to hers.

"I'm sorry about earlier." A weak smile tugged at her mouth. "But I didn't know what else to do to make you see yourself the way everyone else does."

With his fingertips, he brushed a fallen tendril out of her eyes and then grinned. "You were glorious in your fury, especially naked."

Crossing her arms over her breasts, she giggled. "Kind of hard to take me serious like this."

"No. Not at all." He tucked the errant lock of her hair behind her ear. "For a brief moment I thought you planned to kick my ass."

"I have to admit I did think about." She snaked her arms around his neck. "But I'd rather be doing this." Pulling him down, she kissed him and then she grew quiet again, while he moved on to nuzzle her neck.

"Clancy?"

"Hmmm?"

"I know you're going through hell right now, but—"

He tensed, his lips stilling while he waited for her to continue.

"No one can make you believe in yourself. You have to do that on your own. I just want to make it clear that I believe in you."

He inhaled a deep breath, bringing her scent inside him, allowing it to calm him. "Thank you." This woman saw so much, she knew him so much better than he'd imagined.

"I really didn't do anything."

"Darlin', you made me realize that I'm not my father. The truth is, I couldn't do what he had done throughout his life and live with myself. That's apparent to me now."

Her full lips curved slightly. "Do you mean it?"

"Yes. I don't know how I'll ever repay you for forcing me to see the truth."

She snuggled closer. "I might have a couple of suggestions."

"And I'm eager to hear them." He thrust his firming cock into her side, thankful he hadn't removed the condom he put on while she lay across his kitchen table.

"Oh my. You are eager."

Clancy tugged her upright and she threw back her head, laughing. The sweet sound was music to his ears. An unexpected but not unwelcome tenderness welled inside him. That's when he realized he'd fallen for this woman.

"Straddle me."

When her warm, wet sex cradled him, he grew even harder and more aroused. A slight adjustment of her hips and she took him so deep into her sex he closed his eyes. Pleasure, hot and fierce, surged through his veins and he groaned.

It amazed him how perfectly they fit together. Would a life with her be perfect too?

Then she began to move, setting a slow, sensual pace that stole his breath. Lifting his heavy eyelids, he savored the way her body swayed as she rode him. Thrilled with the way her eyes darkened in arousal. And loved the way her lips parted on a sexy, soft mewl.

When her fingernails dug into his chest and bittersweet pain curled through him, he reached for her and took her mouth with a deep, intimate kiss. A kiss so passionate it engraved her name into his heart.

Hands at her waist, he raised her, withdrew slowly, then drove her down hard on his shaft, pushing deep again.

She screamed, "Clancy" as her eyes closed and her back arched. A full-body shiver rippled through her, along his length.

"Not yet," he groaned.

But the radiating tingles wouldn't stop. They teased and threatened to drive him crazy. Grinding his teeth, he fought to hold on, to drag out the moment as long as possible. But it was already too late.

The next spasm of her climax fisted his dick, squeezed and pulled down on his testicles, filling his cock with liquid fire. As he teetered on the point of no return, a throb raced down the inside of his legs to his toes, curling them. His skin tightened. He bucked beneath her and the gates of his control swung open.

"Tess!"

The explosive eruption that surged through him dimmed his vision. Turned him inside out, until breathing didn't matter and only the magic flowing between them did.

Exhausted and vibrating with tremendous physical and mental satisfaction, he pulled her to him. Their hot bodies were deliciously moist. Their hearts pounded in unison. The scent of sex filling the room was a heady aphrodisiac. When he caught his breath, he planned to take her again, but for now he was happy just to lie quietly beneath her.

"Mmmm..." Her sated sound whispered in his ear.

He smiled. For the first time, Clancy was looking forward to the future. A future he hoped included Tess.

As time went by, the events of the day intruded upon him. "I thought she left me." He didn't realize he spoke aloud, until she replied.

"Your mother?"

His throat tightened.

Year after year, her absence, her non-communication, had slowly eaten at him, made him feel as if he wasn't worthy of love. "I thought she didn't care. That maybe she couldn't love me because I was like him." He had never told a soul about his feelings of abandonment, not even Jessie.

Tess nuzzled his neck. "She was your mother, Clancy. She cared, but..." She didn't finish her thought, because she didn't have to.

His father had killed her.

As tension crawled across his skin, he eased from beneath Tess and moved to sit on the edge of the bed, surprised when she crawled behind him, her legs straddled each side of his. Her arms circled his chest. She laid her cheek on his back. Her warmth lending him the support he desperately needed. She held him quietly.

"I should have known."

"How could you?"

"From the moment she disappeared I've had nightmares that he killed her. Subconsciously, I must have known."

"I think those nightmares have come to an end."

God. He hoped so.

"I need to get some pictures from the attic for the sheriff. Will you help me?" He didn't want to face his mother's memory alone.

"Of course, but later." Her silky palms smoothed across his skin. Her lips touched his shoulder with soft kisses. "Now come back to bed. Let me make you forget for a little longer."

And that's exactly what she did. All. Night. Long.

Chapter Twenty

It took almost a week for Clancy's mother's body to be released for burial. Heels sinking into the soft ground, Tess blotted her moist eyes with a tissue as the preacher finished the eulogy. To say the last seven days hadn't been difficult would be a lie.

Clancy's quiet strength had shattered the second they stepped into the attic and he gazed upon a large portrait of his mom. Tess had never seen a grown man cry. As she held him, his sorrow had nearly killed her. Somehow she knew that his outburst had been long overdue. Afterwards he confirmed her suspicion. He had never wept for the loss of his parents. He had been too angry with them.

The ruling of murder, blunt-force trauma to the head, at the hands of his father, hadn't been any easier on Clancy, nor had choosing a cemetery. One thing he was adamant about, his mother wouldn't spend the rest of eternity buried next to his father.

Yet when it came to funeral arrangements, Clancy had been at loose ends. At his side, Tess helped him, but it hadn't been easy for her or her siblings. Too much of their own loss had surfaced, making them all feel raw and vulnerable. But she was proud of her brother and sisters. Even now, they surrounded Clancy as one of their own.

Clancy squeezed her hand before he walked away and placed a white rose on the exquisite light orchid casket with silver handles adorned with pink roses. For a moment, he just stood there. A quiver shook his body, and then he turned back and walked into her waiting arms.

From experience she knew the service was an important part of the grieving process, a time to say good-bye—Clancy's time.

When he raised his head and a weak smile touched his lips, she knew he would be all right. As he stepped beside her, he reached for her hand. Together they watched his mother's casket drift down and disappear beneath the earth.

The plot he had chosen lay beneath a large pine tree and for a moment she listened to the wind whisper through the branches. An ocean of emerald green spread across acre after acre of land. Large, mature trees aligned the perimeter and were dotted throughout the cemetery. A beautiful and peaceful resting place meant for someone who had been loved very much.

It would take nearly two weeks for the mortuary to install the marble headstone he'd chosen. The matching bench she suggested that would be placed not more than five feet away would be set tomorrow. It was important to have a place to come when the thoughts of a loved one rose.

This time she squeezed his hand. "You okay?"

"I am now. She's finally at rest." He didn't say any more, because a barrage of people began to approach him.

Something close to panic widened his eyes, but her family closed in around him like bodyguards, allowing only one or two at a time to invade his space. While Wade shook his hand, Jessie pulled Tess into her embrace.

"Thank you for being here for him." She stepped away from Tess and newfound tears glistened in her eyes. "I told you he was worth it."

And the woman had been right.

It took nearly an hour for people to say their condolences.

"I can't believe there are so many people." He seemed overwhelmed by the amount of compassion coming his way.

"Is it so hard to accept that people care about you—love you, like I do?" The admission tumbled from her mouth before she realized it. When his expression went blank, Tess wished she could take it back, but what was done was done.

His mouth opened, but before he could respond, a woman in her forties stepped up and introduced herself. "I met your mother at the safe house just before her death. All she could talk about was getting back to you—" She swallowed nervously and glanced toward the open grave. "Getting you out of that situation."

Tess started to step away, give them privacy, but he grabbed her hand and pulled her to his side.

His grip tightened. "Thank you, Ms. White."

"Call me Ellen." Then she leaned in to him and gave him a hug. "She loved you very much. Don't ever doubt that."

As she released him, Clancy cleared his throat. When he sniffled, Tess knew he struggled with his emotions.

"Ellen, please feel free to join us at Clancy's house." Tess moved closer to him. "We're having a bite to eat."

"Thank you, but I best be getting home." She smiled, then turned and walked away.

"You ready to go?" Tess asked.

"Yeah. Let's get out of here."

The limousine ride back to his house took place in silence. Arm slung across her shoulders, he played absentmindedly with the lace on her short-sleeved black dress, while she gazed out the window. Exhaustion slipped into her bones and she wondered if admitting her feelings had frightened him.

As they pulled into the driveway, Levi and the girls awaited them. The driver didn't even have the opportunity to open the door before Levi grasped the handle and gave it a pull. Like a gentleman he helped her out.

"Hey, Wiseman." He grinned. "Just heard that prize Gelbvieh bull of yours jumped the fence again." Clancy groaned, but Levi's smile grew larger. "Seems he's been doing the dirty with a couple of our cows."

If it hadn't been that she had kept Levi busy from sun up until now, Tess might think her little brother had a hand in the bull's release. Still, she couldn't help the excitement that touched her. It was their future plans to crossbreed. This just gave them a huge leap in that direction with a quality animal they could never afford.

"Damn animal." Clancy glanced from Levi to her. "You don't look all broken up about my cattle on your property this time."

"I guess we could take you to court for damages," she teased.

"Damages, my ass. You know what one of his calves are worth?"

Levi burst into laughter as the girls giggled behind him.

Rachel wrapped an arm around Tess's waist. "Everything is ready."

While Levi and Clancy chatted, Tess and the girls went into the house. The first person she met was Milo, his beautiful dark-haired daughter beside him.

Concern heavy in his eyes, he extended a hand and shook Tess's. "How is he?"

"As well as one can be on a day like this, but I think he'll be okay. How are the two of you doing?" They had been in their new place for a week now.

Love beamed in the man's eyes as he looked down upon his daughter. "We're good. Julie, why don't you join Rose and Rachel in the kitchen." When the girl scampered off, Milo's voice lowered. "Her momma has agreed to me having full custody for now. Seems she's hooked up with another man." The brilliance that once brightened his gaze disappeared.

She gave him a big hug. "These things have a way of working out. You'll see." Men like Milo and Clancy wouldn't stay single for long.

The thought hardly tweaked her mind when Clancy stepped into the house. For the first time he appeared relaxed. From the small tidbits she heard of his, Levi and Wade's conversation, all the work on the new property was done. A monument had been erected where his mother had been found. Tomorrow they would be releasing both Wiseman and Gilmore cattle on the land. Levi had insisted on paying grazing rights and Tess couldn't have been prouder of him.

As more and more people poured into the house, the noise level soared. A group of men now surrounded Clancy, each of them holding a beer in their hands. In another room she heard laughter and the smash of billiards crashing together.

This was exactly what Clancy needed. She took one more look at the handsome man, and then drifted toward the kitchen to make sure everything was running smoothly when she saw Levi and Tori slip out the front door.

The girl must have had a homing device on her, because all three of her brother's heads rose at the same time, their troubled gazes drawn to the door that clicked shut. Wade said something to Clint and Ty and the two brothers headed for the door.

Tess started to follow, slowing her steps. Maybe it was time for her brother to stand on his own two feet. She pivoted and then paused. They wouldn't hurt Levi, would they? "Nah," she said before continuing on her way.

After everyone left, Clancy collapsed upon the couch and toed off his boots. What had started as an emotionally charged day had evolved into a gathering of friends and family he never realized he had. Even his workhands pitched in to make the day easier on him and for that he was thankful. Still, he owed most of his gratitude to one woman.

Tess.

Her strength and compassion helped him through this very trying day and those that had followed his mother's discovery. He gazed up at the portrait above the fireplace of a smiling woman with haunting eyes, eyes so like his own.

What would she look like today if his father hadn't snatched her life away?

A memory of her sitting on the edge of his bed and reading *The Little Rabbit Who Wanted Red Wings* came softly. Like the rabbit, he hadn't been happy—prayed to be somebody else. Was that another thing they had in common? Had she quietly recited the same prayer night after night?

Why had it taken him so long to see the truth about himself? So many years had been wasted, but no more. He had a long way to go to break old habits and fears, but from this point onward he would live his life the way it should be lived. Hopefully his life would include Tess, her brother and sisters. He was ready for the whole enchilada.

Closing his eyes, he leaned back and rested his head on the back of the leather couch. For a brief moment his mind went blank and peace filled the silence. When his eyelids rose, Tess stood over him like she had that first night they met.

"Are you an angel?"

She shook her head. "Far from it."

But she had been his saving grace—his angel.

He held out his hand. "Will you be my angel tonight?" When she intertwined her fingers with his, he pulled her down beside him. Her dress hiked up to midthigh, revealing black nylon-covered legs so inviting he couldn't help reaching out and feeling the silk beneath his touch. When his hand slipped between her knees, she locked them together.

Raising a brow, she forced a smile that didn't quite make it to her eyes, eyes that appeared weary. "You really need to get some new pickup lines."

Cupping the back of her head, he urged her mouth to his, but he didn't kiss her. "You are an angel, Tess. Thank you for today and the last week."

And for saving me from self-destruction and loving me.

He'd nearly swallowed his tongue when she had revealed her feelings earlier. He had wanted to take her in his arms, kiss her, and tell her that he loved her, but they had been interrupted. He wanted to be alone with her when he expressed his love. The only woman, besides Jessie, that he'd ever loved.

"You're welcome. I finished cleaning up the kitchen and put all the food away. You'll have enough to last you a month. Do you want me to fix you something before I leave?"

"I'm not hungry, not for food."

Surprisingly, he didn't want a drink either. No. He wanted something more primitive, more carnal. He wanted to feast on her mouth and body. Feel her naked skin sliding across his. See her beautiful face when she climaxed.

Her cheeks blushed.

"Stay with me, Tess."

"Uhm...I really shouldn't." She worried her bottom lip with her teeth. "Levi and the girls expect me home."

He brushed his mouth over hers. "Please stay."

"Maybe I can until you fall asleep."

"Perhaps I'm not making my position clear. I don't need someone to kiss me goodnight and tuck me in." He gazed into the depths of her eyes. "And I don't want you to stay for just tonight, but every night. I want to wake up with you in my arms every morning."

She eased back, angling her shoulders away from him. "What are you saying?"

"I'm saying I love you. I want you—a family." The revelation came easily, shocking him as well as Tess. Her jaw dropped. Her eyes widened.

"Clancy, are you sure? I come with a lot of baggage."

"We all do. Mine is a bit different from yours. At least your baggage will grow up, go to college, and marry. I can deal with that." He smoothed his nose against hers. "And who knows, maybe we'll create some baggage of our own."

She licked her lips. "You want children?"

"I want to share everything life has to offer with you, and that includes children. We'll have a houseful of them if that's what you want." He slid the sleeve of her dress off a shoulder, pressed his mouth against her soft skin and nibbled. Then he looked up through shuttered eyelids. "You might even be able to convince me to begin trying for our first piece of baggage tonight."

She leaned into him. "I *might* be able to?" Her voice lowered to a sexy purr.

Did this mean—

His heart rate quickened. "So, darlin', will you marry me?"

She threw her arms around his neck, knocked him back against the couch, and peppered his face with kisses. "Yes." Her voice pitched as her response came in rapid succession. "Yes. Yes. Yes."

His foolish grin died and he choked up a bit at the sudden emotion dampening her eyes. Gently he brushed away what he hoped were happy tears now rolling down her cheeks.

"Tess?" Leaning closer, he kissed the corners of her lips and the tip of her nose. "I'll make you happy. I promise."

Her warm palms cupped his face. "You already make me happy. But there is something that would make me even happier right now."

"Anything. You name it and it's yours."

"Take me to bed. And, Clancy?"

"Yes."

A sensual smile curved her lips. "Can we use those handcuffs from the other night?"

"Oh hell yeah." He grabbed her hand, dragging her up and into his embrace when he stood. "Anything else you want?"

"Hmmm..." Her voice softened. "Only you."

When their mouths touched in a poignant kiss that tightened his chest, Clancy knew he'd found the woman who could truly complete him.

About the Author

A taste of the erotic, a measure of daring and a hint of laughter describe Mackenzie McKade's novels. She sizzles the pages with scorching sex, fantasy and deep emotion that will touch you and keep you immersed until the end. Whether her stories are contemporaries, futuristics or fantasies, this Arizona native thrives on giving you the ultimate erotic adventure.

When not traveling through her vivid imagination, she's spending time with three beautiful daughters, three devilishly handsome grandsons, and the man of her dreams. She loves to write, enjoys reading, and can't wait till summer. Boating and jet skiing are top on her list of activities. Add to that laughter and if mischief is in order—Mackenzie's your gal!

To learn more about Mackenzie McKade, please visit mackenziemckade.com. Send an email to Mackenzie at mackenzie@mackenziemckade.com or catch her on the following:

Facebook: facebook.com/MackenzieMcKade

Twitter: @MackenzieMcKade

Yahoo: groups.yahoo.com/group/macsdreamscape

www.samhainpublishing.com

Green for the planet.
Great for your wallet.

It's all about the story...

Romance

HORROR

www.samhainpublishing.com

CPSIA information can be obtained at www.ICGtesting.com
Printed in the USA
BVOW04s0923250314

348701BV00004B/95/P